Minnie Piper

Undercover

Puzzler

To the fabaroony Juskus boys, who protect
me from all things scaly on the planet.

STRIPES PUBLISHING
An imprint of Magi Publications
1 The Coda Centre, 189 Munster Road, London SW6 6AW

A paperback original
First published in Great Britain in 2006

Text copyright © Caroline Juskus, 2006
Illustrations copyright © Kate Leake, 2006

ISBN-10:1-84715-011-X
ISBN-13: 978-1-84715-011-0

A CIP catalogue record for this book is available from the British Library.

Printed in Belgium by Proost

2 4 6 8 10 9 7 5 3 1

STARRING

Minnie Piper

undercover

Puzzler

caroline
Juskus

Illustrated by
Kate Leake

Stripes

My name is Minnie and my speciality is doodling poems; but

I am also a secret undercover puzzler

Never say NEVER is my mum's favourite expression which gets on my

$3x + 4 = 12$

Nerves because

i need to say things like, "I never

ever like doing HOMEWORK."

Peculiarly though, Mr

Impey, my new teacher, has set us homework that is

Probably my best homework

Ever. This is a miracle as homework and me are a little bit like

Rice Krispies and ketchup and should never EVER mix!

This is my homework:

```
vpmhtsyi;syopmd ejprbrt
upi str/ gpt nromh dp
v;rbrt smf vtsvlomh yjr
vpfr yjrtr od s yep [pimf vpom
pm yp[ pg yjr v;pvl nu
yjr npstf/ hp smf hry oy/
oy od upit DRVTRY SHRMY [toxr/
```

It is a TOP SECRET CODED MESSAGE! And the first one to crack it wins a prize!

I cannot believe it, but for the first time ever I spookily have homework that I actually like. And being a secret undercover puzzler, I am hoping for once to beat Brainiac Jenny, the cleverest girl in the whole of the universe (and my class). I am desperate to start puzzling the code... NOW! Not in a minute or an hour, or tomorrow. But right NOW! This very instant! But there's one very BIG problem that stands in my way, and it comes in the shape of one very small person ... my cling-on cousin DOT!

TUESDAY AFTER SCHOOL

Cling-on Dot!

Dot tells everyone she is five and three-quarters, which is really and truly only five, and as I am ten (and eleven-twelfths), it is not exactly overly cool to have a whimpering snip of a cousin acting like she's my *Shadow*. But that's what she does. She clings to my side like a fridge to a magnet and whenever I manage to peel her away she simply springs back on.

I used to only see her for birthdays, but 17 days, five hours and ten minutes ago (not that I'm counting), she moved into Wayne Parker's old flat in Block A, Arthurs Way. Sadly I live in Block B, Arthurs Way, so now I live one block from a cling-on and have to see her all the time. She's endlessly sniffing and goes on and on about her old house and her old school and her old friends and her old bedroom. But most of all she goes on about missing her mum, Aunty Valerie, who has gone to France and left Dot with Uncle Jeff.

"BOING"

I do feel the teensiest bit sorry for Dot, but much more ENORMOUSLY sorry for <u>ME</u> because Uncle Jeff always has to work late, which leaves me as chief babysitter. And I am probably about to pull out my hair because for the eighth torturous night in a row, that is what I am doing now … when I should be solving a code!

☆　　　　　　　☆

Dot is fidgeting on our bright pink sofa, and she is upside down with her head on the seat where her bottom should be, and her legs are climbing up the back. This is annoying as I am sitting the right way up, but then I try it and it is actually, peculiarly good at making the TV a lot more interesting. Dot giggles when I tell her this and says, "I love your Pink sofa, Minnie, because I love Pink. And your flat is just like a RAINBOW

And this is true, because Mum's speciality is painting Dad's wacky furniture designs in need-your-sunglasses dazzling colours. Like the bright yellow sideboard with no handles so that it's nearly impossible to get inside it, but is particularly good at holding the telly. And the hanging dining table that is strung from the ceiling in the corner of our sitting-room on four long ropes. Mum has painted it bright orange, with pink spots where the plates should sit, and when you put your elbows on it, it greedily swings your dinner away. Dad says it's a good-manners-teaching table, because all good children should know never to put their elbows on a table.

Dot and I are still upside down and trying to watch an art programme and the presenter is making a giant picture of a footballer out of football socks and shirts. Dot gets fed up and sniffs, "I don't do football, Minnie."

"It isn't football, Dot," I say. "It is making a picture, which just so happens to be about football."

"I don't do football pictures," sniffs Dot. "Especially Wayne Parker's football pictures in my horrid bedroom. It isn't fair! Dad said he would paint my room Pink, but he never has any time."

And all of this is non-fibbing true, and for once I am actually on Dot's side, because Dot's new bedroom is totally blue and a shrine to football which Wayne Parker left behind. And her walls and curtains say CHELSEA FC forever and for the zillionth time today I wish Uncle Jeff wouldn't work so late and then he'd have time to paint Dot's room. This might stop Dot moaning so much and I wouldn't have to keep babysitting and I might have time to work on the secret code. And most important of all – I could spend more time with Frankie Minelli, my best-ever friend.

But I don't tell Dot this and, fed up with football pictures, she stomps off in MY BEST boots, to help Mum in the kitchen. Dad comes in, and I tell him, "Dot is totally getting on my nerves." And I don't know if it's because I'm upside down but it just slips out before I can think, "And Frankie says Aunty Valerie must be horrid as she's gone to France and left Dot, and all the French eat is frogs' legs and snails."

Dad looks serious for a very rare moment and says, "Aunty Valerie isn't horrid, it's just that it's hard to be a grown-up sometimes. Especially a grown-up with not much money."

"But what about only eating snails?"

"They're delicious," he grins. "It's the garlic that does it. And that reminds me. What d'you call a slug in a crash helmet?"

I refuse to answer. But he tells me anyway, "A snail of course!" And he is just about to tell me another with, "And what's the difference between a snail and a gobstopper?" when thankfully...

"Tea time!" hollers Mum, as she wheels in Spike, my one-year-old wiggly, wriggly brother, in his tiger-striped high chair.

"...You can't chew on a gobstopper!" giggles Dad.

And excuse me while I might be sick, because if it's not stomach-churning bad hearing Dad's jokes, or facing Mum's healthy-option tea of nut rissoles and easy-peasy-cheesy lentils, then it must be stomach-churning bad to chew garlic snails!

Dot sits next to me, and stares at her plate, and she is so upset by what's for tea that she slumps her elbows on to the table, and forgets it's what all good

11

children must never do. The table swings her tea away and Dot slips and nearly lands with her head in her food. Dad laughs, but my plate has nearly tipped in my lap and now I'm not in my friendliest mood. Dot sniffs, "I don't do easy-peasy lentils."

And neither, it seems, does tadpole Spike, because he's wriggling as usual and spitting out lentils as fast as Mum can shovel them in. The table stops swinging and somehow I find myself grumbling to Dot, "NOBODY willingly does ANY sort of lentils, easy-peasy-cheesy or not! But lentils are fibrously better than snails, which is probably what your mum is eating because that's what they eat in France!"

"Minnie!" say Dad and Mum together.

And I know I've done wrong, so I say, "Peculiarly, snails are delicious, Dot – it's the garlic that does it, so you should be happy and not sad."

But Dot is blubbing and Dad marches me off to my room and says, "YOU might be crying if your mum was in France. We must all be trying to help one another."

And I want to say that Dot is trying. VERY TRYING! But Dad's lecturing me with, "It's a difficult time for Dot right now, what with having a new home and a new school. And Uncle Jeff worries she's missing her mum."

And now I feel bad and promise I will try to be nicer to Dot, so Dad says I can go back to my lentils, and I wonder if this is the best of rewards for someone who's trying to be good.

This is my try-to-be-nice-to-Dot plan: after tea I let her show me her wobbly tooth. Then I challenge her to Snakes and Ladders and let her win, even though she goes *up* the snakes and *down* the ladders.

And then we play with Wanda Wellingtons, my totally loopy, fluffy Jack Russell, and when Mum suggests that she might like a walk, I very nicely let Dot hold the lead while we make plans for her new bedroom. Dot wants a princess bed with a pink eiderdown (which is just a duvet if you're not a princess), and pink everywhere you can absolutely think of, like even the carpet beneath the bed and the insides of her wardrobe. But I say purple would probably, definitely be better, with lavender walls and lilac carpet and purple netting hanging from the ceiling from a sparkling crown, to drape, princess-like, either side of her bed.

"I don't do purple," sniffs Dot, unimpressed.

"Oh," I sigh. "Well I'll probably think up something better as soon as we get back home."

However, the very moment I kick off my boots and sit back down on the *Pink* sofa, with *Pink* spotty cushions, all I can think of is *Pink*. So we play h a n g m a n and Dot hangs me because she cannot spell and she doesn't understand what hangman is. And after an hour of I Spy, where Dot thinks that ceiling begins with S, and every other word is M E (which stands for Mrs Elliott, Dot's teacher, who has never, ever been in our flat, let alone twenty-seven times in one evening!), I am just trying to explain, "It is probably best to think up new words, Dot, and preferably of something I can actually see," when FINALLY Uncle Jeff comes to my rescue.

He is puffing, having run up the stairs to the flat, and though he is always in jogging trousers, he is not exactly the jogging type. But he's definitely a much better joker than Dad, and he smiles at us from his fat pink face and giggles, "Sorry I'm late, but I could have been later ... so technically, I am still early! ...And how's my little Polka Dotty?" (He always calls Dot "Polka Dotty", not because she likes polka dots, but because a polka is a kind of dance and Dotty is a kind of dancer.)

"OK," sniffs Dot, as he twirls her about like a mad circus pony. And then they bow most politely and trot out the door with Dot shouting, "Bye, Minnie. See you tomorrow."

"Bye," I sigh, as I look at my watch and see that it's almost nine o'clock. Mum says it is time for bed but I just have a moment to ring Frankie and complain that Dot has only just gone.

"For someone so tiny, Dot is proving a *HUGE* nuisance," says Frankie.

"*GiNORMOUS*," I grumble. But it's hard to say more when Mum is stood over me tapping her watch. I just manage to ask Frankie if she's cracked the code.

Frankie laughs and says, "No way, *Poodle Noodle*!"

And, with that good news, it's time for bed.

TUESDAY NIGHT

Lost at sea

I know I should go straight to sleep, but I don't get homework I like very often, especially homework that comes with a prize! So I decide to risk it and stay up late and pretend I'm a secret spy on a mission and this is what I'm doing now EXCEPT...

"Minnie Minx, are you in bed yet?"

...I keep on getting interrupted!

"Yes, Mum. I'm very in bed." And I'm telling the truth because I am in bed. I'm just not in bed in my hideous nightie, that is much too small, and age 7-8, with a picture of Tigger bouncing on the front (when I'm clearly ten and nearly eleven and Mum doesn't seem to have sussed this yet). And nor am I in my Princess pyjamas because the *elastic* has broken and when

I stand **up** the trousers fall **d o w n** and I have to pull them on at the very last moment.

So I am IN bed, but not actually ready for bed, as I'm still in my funky caterpillars (stripy tights in shades of purple), denim skirt, and a T-shirt that I'm wearing inside out so that no one can read it says "I'm cute", and I haven't a millisecond for removing clothes. Instead, I am secretly shining the green-glowing head of my alien pen spookily over the code...

```
vpmhtsyi;syopmd  ejprbrt
upi  str/  gpt  nromh  dp
v;rbrt  smf  vtsvlomh  yjr
vpfr  yjrtr  od  s  yep [pimf  vpom
pm  yp[  pg  yjr  v;pvl  nu
yjr  npstf/  hp  smf  hry  oy/
oy  od  upit  DRVTRY  SHRMY [toxr/
```

It looks a bit tricky, but I happen to know a lot about codes because when Mum's at work I usually go to Gran's for tea and help her with her *Puzzling Times*, which is a kind of comic for people who like crosswords more than *The Beano*. I am odd as I like crosswords AND *The Beano*, and I'm specially keen on Minnie the Minx, who takes on anyone and usually wins, and I think of her whenever anyone laughs at my name, or calls me Minnie Mouse. But the *Puzzling Times* is full to bursting with spot-the-difference and word searches and mystery messages and this has taught me a lot about codes, and now I'm really into them.

Or trying to be! Because Dad is shouting, "Are you in bed, Minnie?"

"Yes, Dad."

"Are you actually under the covers?"

"Yes, Dad, I'm under the covers."

And I REALLY AM undercover – under my duvet in my lost-at-sea bedroom, which, just like everything else in our flat, has been painted by my mum: the walls have dolphins swimming all over them, my floor is painted with starfish and coral, and there's even an octopus skulking in a corner. My bed is one of Dad's designs and made of poles lashed together so that it looks like a raft afloat at sea. And my duvet has dolphins diving all over it and right now I am snuggled beneath it so I can truthfully say I am under the covers! Well, as Gran says, "If you need to puzzle something important, dear, always do it undercover. It's what all the very best puzzlers do."

And Gran should know. She's the best puzzler ever and her speciality is anagrams, where you have to make a word out of jumbled up letters. They do it on a programme called Spellbound on the telly and Gran is in love with Johnny Sprightly, the man in charge of the scoring. I don't know why, because he wears absolutely terrible ties, but Gran goes pink and squishy and gooey, a little bit like a strawberry cream, whenever anyone whispers his name. On Valentine's Day Dad sent her a card and signed it,

yours adoringly,

♡ *Johnny Sprightly* ♡
                                                     x x x

Gran said she knew it was from Dad, but it still made her heart flutter.

Anyway, I know the code isn't anagrams because there aren't enough vowels, so I'm turning all the A's into B's, and B's into C's and C's into D's right up to Z, and then you turn the Z into A.

But I don't know what to do with [or / and anyway, my answer's not right because…

wqniutzj;tzpqne fkqscSu vqj tus/
hqu ospni eq w;scsu tng wutwmpni
zks wgqgs zksus pe t zfq [qjng
wqpn qn zq[qah zks Wiqwm ov
zks oqtug/ iq tng isz pz/ pz
pe vqju eswusz tisnz [upys/

...doesn't make any sense.

It's so maddeningly peculiar because there are semi-colons in the middle of words, and I don't actually know what semi-colons do even if they're in the right place. I decide to act upon another piece of advice from Gran, which is, "To solve a puzzle it is a good idea to know your puzzler". For example, if he or she who has set the puzzle just happens to be a food fanatic, then the puzzle is probably all about food. And if they happen to be mad on cats then you are probably, definitely, purrfectly right to think that cats are the answer.

Mr Impey, my teacher who set the code, just happens to be a trampoliner so maybe he's set us a bouncy code and you have to jump from letter to letter!

Or it could be to do with World War II, as that's our new project and Mr Impey knows lots about it. But I can't be sure and I'm now so tired that my brain is scrambled and tied in a tangle and if I don't shut my eyes in the next ten seconds they are going to close all by themselves.

I stuff my alien pen under my mattress and can only hope that Brainiac Jenny has been just as distracted and has had to do heaps of book-reading practice. And I know I shouldn't want to beat my best friend Frankie, but she's always so much more perfect than me that for once I secretly do.

I wriggle out of my funky caterpillars and slide my legs into my no-elastic pyjamas and begin on my second code of the night. This is my code to Wanda Wellingtons, and it is not written down, and is truly more of a secret signal: I drum my fingers on my bedroom wall (which is the wall that divides my room from the kitchen, which may sound odd if you live in a house, but I live in a flat and all the rooms are next to each other), and then Wanda sneaks in like a secret agent, gives me a look for the all clear, which I confirm by giving my next secret signal, which is patting my duvet three times. Then

Wanda jumps up and licks my face and curls herself into a furry ball at the bottom of my quilt. I whisper, "Minnie to Wanda, over and out," (which means I know she is tired and ready for bed), and Wanda's signal is to close her eyes... ...and we both drift off to sleep.

And tonight I dream...
...I have cracked the code and this is what it says:

Minnie Piper, you are spookily brilliant and have won the undercover puzzler's prize. And the prize is. . .

WEDNESDAY AT SCHOOL

Behind the pet shed

On the way to this morning's assembly I tell Frankie about my dream.

"What was the prize?" whispers Frankie. (We must NOT speak on our way to assembly, and we must NOT run or pick our noses. Other than that we can have bags of fun and be mind-numbingly sensible and yawningly boring.)

"That's the trouble, I don't know," I whisper back. "Dad woke me JUST at the moment I was about to find out, to tell me that my breakfast was ready. And if I didn't get to the table in precisely, and exactly, fifteen seconds my Rice Krispies would self-destruct and instead of snapping and crackling and popping they would be soggily sticking to the roof of my mouth and squelching like frogspawn on the tip of my tongue."

"Yuck," squeals Frankie. "Unlucky! Frogspawn for breakfast AND you didn't get your prize."

"Being unlucky is my speciality," I sigh.

And very unluckily I get caught for whispering,

and have to stand throughout assembly. And it is beetrooty embarrassing because people like Trevor and Tiffany stare at you and you are not allowed to stare back or Grumpy Hooper, our head teacher, makes you stand for A WHOLE WEEK. Even though it is Frankie who squealed, it is me who goes and gets caught red-handed. But Frankie is like that: sparklingly lucky. And I am not. I am shampoo-in-your-eyes UNlucky.

So here I am, stood in assembly, when everyone else is sitting on the floor, and now I know how a giraffe feels because I'm so much taller than everyone else. Grumpy is droning on about being polite, and very politely, so as not to yawn, I completely ignore him till assembly has finished, and then we snake our way back to class and the good news is that no one, not even Brainiac Jenny, definitely knows they have cracked the code.

All apart from Trevor, who insists it says: "I win double portions of chips for the rest of my life and am excused from homework for ever!"

Mr Impey is very impressed and jumps up and down in his peacock-blue tracksuit and says, "Master Bottomley, you may have unearthed a miraculous code-cracking cell in your brain and found a message so secret that I never ever knew it existed. If you can show me how you did it I will personally buy you double chips."

"Can't," snorts Trevor. "Can't think on an empty stomach. I'll 'ave to tell you when I've 'ad the chips."

"Deal," agrees Mr Impey.

And then we learn our nine times table and I cannot get it right.

☆   ☆   ☆

At lunchtime Frankie and I always sneak outside to eat our lunches behind the pet shed. To do this we have to be super-sleuth secret because all lunches must be eaten in the hall. But when the only seat is next to Trevor, who is chewing pork pies and pickled onion crisps with his mouth open like a cement mixer, there is sadly little choice!

The pet shed is mouse-dropping smelly due to the hamsters and mice inside it, but luckily its pongy odour is just what I need as an excuse to never go in. I've never told anyone, but secretly I am scarily petrified of scaly things, like the feet of birds or the skins of snakes … so scared that my knees turn to jelly and my mouth dries up as if I've gobbled a packet of cream crackers. And the pet shed is full of scaly tails, and scaly feet, and it's my very worst nightmare.

And most annoyingly, so is Frankie's room now! Three months ago her mum bought her hamsters and I'm so nervous that I begin to shake with the thought of each visit. But I'm too afraid to share my secret and have told Frankie I'm a wuss with smells and thankfully she now covers their cage to cut out their whiffy aroma. Yet I'm quite happy behind the pet shed, as it's the perfect place to nibble your lunch, as nobody ever knows that you're there. Frankie and I can hide in secret and think about things like being a dancer/popstar (Frankie) and an undercover puzzler (me).

Today, however, we are thinking about Mr Impey, our wiz new teacher, who has taken over from Grumpy Hooper (who's sadly been promoted to head teacher, or headache, more precisely). Mr Impey is totally chilled. He has five tracksuits and each one is a different colour (colour-coded for every school day) and his hair is sometimes tied into plaits or let loose in a giant Afro. Grumpy hasn't got an Afro. Grumpy's hair is neat and trim and his suit is grey and not at all a tracksuit, and it has a buttoned-up jacket with a white hanky in the top pocket that he uses to mop his brow in assembly when he gets wound up and hot.

Anyway, most peculiarly, when Mr Impey set our secret message homework, he said, "Don't worry if you find it boring... The key to the code is being bored!" Grumpy Hooper would never say this. (Grumpy always tuts if we're bored, and makes us do star jumps until we're UN-bored.) So me and Frankie are behind the pet shed, thinking Year 6 is not as bad as we scarily thought (even though we've only done ten days), and WHY the key to the code is being bored.

"It's probably because it's boring," decides Frankie. "Unlike this!" And she stuffs five olives into her mouth, which is seven short of her record.

"Give you my banana if you squeeze my boiled egg in too!" I offer.

29

"No way!" splutters Frankie.

And I can't blame her because cold boiled eggs and squidgy bananas are not exactly tempting treats when her own lunch consists of lip-smacking *Minellis Deli* pizza and scrummy-yummy died-and-gone-to-heaven chocolate cake from her mum and dad's café and delicatessen.

"Dare you to stare at this for two minutes without blinking then," I challenge, holding up the code.

"Dare you to kiss Trevor for two minutes without blinking if I do," giggles Frankie. And she's just stuck her finger up her nose in an impersonation of Trevor, when...

"Who's Trevor?" sneaks a sniffly voice.

Frankie and I look down and, there like an itch you can't scratch, is my cling-on cousin Dot. She has come to check on her furry friends, and this is count-to-ten annoying as now she has found my secret hideout and lunchtimes are just for me and Frankie, and NOT for me and Frankie and Dot!

I am just about to shoo her away when I decide I'd better count to ten, as Gran advises for heated moments, and I've nearly got to nine and three-quarters as Gran's words come floating back that "blood is thicker than water, dear", which means be nice to your family through **THICK** and t̶hin. And as Dot is my cousin, and I promised Dad I'd try hard to be nice, I try my hardest to smile and say, "Trevor is the very worst boy in the universe and he has sticking-out ears that look even bigger than they probably are on account of his hair being clipped so short, which makes him look like a pair of scissors. Plus he is uselessly late at handing in homework and this is why our class marble pot is always going down not up. This is very annoying because when it is full we're going on a trip and marble winning is a 'team effort', and I HATE team efforts because Trevor is NEVER good at teams, and when he's on a team it's always MY team!"

"Oh," sniffs Dot, probably wishing she'd never asked. And, as irritatingly as a fly on your sandwich, she adds, "Do you want to see me wobble my tooth?"

"No, Dot, I'm eating my lunch!"

So she asks Frankie to teach her to spin and Frankie says, "You're too little. And it's not a spin, it's a pirouette."

"Oh," sniffs Dot. "But I can do the splits."

"Fabaroony," says Frankie. But I can tell she isn't really impressed, and not that keen on Dot either. Dot is taking up bags of my time and getting in the way of me and Frankie being best-ever friends, because instead of seeing each other after school I now have to babysit Dot.

"Frankie and I have homework," I grumble, "which must be very, very boring and is a code for girls who are ten not five."

Dot stands on her toes and says, "I am very nearly ten."

And I say, "Sadly, not very nearly enough."

Dot's bottom lip begins to tremble so I generously give her my last Marmite sandwich, which cheers her up because she loves Marmite like she loves hamsters, and she skips away to hide in a corner.

"I've got loads of cousins," says Frankie, as Dot disappears, "but thankfully they're all still in Italy. I used to be sad that I never see them, but imagine if they were all like Dot!"

"AND you had to share your gran with them. It's just my UNluck that my gran is Dot's gran! I wish she'd gone to France with her mum, but Dad says Aunty Valerie needs some 'me time', which means she needs to be on her own. She's a bit depressed because she used to be earning squillions of money and buying everyone really nice things, like a purple glittery hairbrush for me and a gigantic house for Uncle Jeff. Then she lost her job and they had to sell their gigantic house and live in Arthurs Way. The thought of it has sent her mad, what with the noise, and neighbours like Trevor, so she's gone to France to stay with a friend until she's feeling better."

"What if she never feels better?" groans Frankie. "Then I'll be stuck with a cling-on forever."

"Unlucky ... but horrid Aunty Valerie would be stuck with ... horrid garlic snails forever!"

"Maybe. But Dad said Aunty Valerie AND snails are not THAT horrid! And I think he's right because she's always been nice and before she left she gave me a book of revolting rhymes as a present for helping Uncle Jeff with Dot."

"But what about the revolting snails?"

"Perhaps you should eat one to find out!"

"Or make up a revolting snail rhyme! Come on, Minnie, let's do one now."

"OK." And this is what I like about Frankie. She

is very good at thinking up things … even if they are disgusting! And we are just wondering what rhymes with snail when, unpoetically, the bell goes and Mr Impey is blowing his whistle and we have to line up behind Terrible Trevor, who is revolting whether he rhymes or not. He is sticking his fingers into his sticking-out ears and picking out wax and moulding it into tiny balls that he's flicking at the back of Tiffany Me-Me's head.

☆ ☆ ☆

When we get back into class, Mr Impey asks Trevor if he can now explain the code. But Trevor says he can't because the double chips were so greasy that all his secret code information has slipped from his mind, and it's all Mr Impey's fault!

And the thought of Trevor's earwax and double chips, and Aunty Valerie stuffing herself with garlic snails, makes me feel queasy all afternoon. Especially when Mr Impey starts teaching us about rationing. Trevor writes this down as "rasherning", and is amusing himself by drawing a pig being rashered into bacon.

"Don't look!" squeals Frankie, and I try not to, but Trevor is now adding stomach-churning detail with a bright red pen, and it is can't-tear-your-eyes-away hard NOT to look when the real rationing is mind numbingly boring and just about sharing out teaspoons of sugar. And to make matters worse, Mr Impey is showing us a tin of dried eggs, and it's what they had to eat in the war, and we have to sniff it and it smells like Spike's nappies.

I'm still feeling sick when it's time to go home.

PURE DRIED
EGGS

WEDNESDAY AFTER SCHOOL

Never ever kiss a Trevor!

At long last the bell goes and me and Frankie grab our things and run to meet Gran, who's in the playground, waiting to take us home. Maddeningly, she is also taking Dot home and Dot, as always, is late. Frankie and I are keen to get going, especially as I have a night off from Dot, so Gran says, "If you promise to be careful dear, you and Frankie can walk back on your own. Four eyes are better than two!"

And before it's too late, and Dot arrives, we scoot off across the playground, Frankie swinging her violin in her violin-shaped case, and me swinging a carrier bag saying **BARGAIN BANANAS**, because my backpack has broken and Mum hasn't thought to mend it yet, or even buy me a new one.

When we get home Mum is in the kitchen and Frankie says, "Hi, Mrs Piper." (She never calls Mum Audrey, which totally sadly is Mum's name, and when I tell Frankie that she's SO lucky to have parents called Violetta and Fabio, Frankie NEVER says, "Rubbish! Audrey and Malcolm are fabaroony names." She just nibbles her nails and hovers in silence and waits for me to say something new.)

"Hi, Minnie-and-Frankie United," cheers Mum. (At my place we're Minnie-and-Frankie Utd and at Frankie's we're Frankie-and-Minnie Utd.) "Had a good day then?"

"Average," I mumble. "It was bad in that we had to do our nine times table, and good in that no one has cracked the code."

"Except for Trevor," giggles Frankie. "But he ate too many chips and it slipped his mind."

"Oh dear," smiles Mum. "Well, I'm no good with codes, but I could help you with your nine times table."

"No thanks," I tell her.

And then Dad pokes his head round the kitchen door and smiles, "I could help you with your nine times table."

"NO!" I scream. "I've done enough maths today to last me a lifetime." And before they can multiply and come out of the woodwork screaming, "MATHS! MATHS! MATHS!" I desperately make a grab for Frankie and pull her into my bedroom.

"Shall we hide?" giggles Frankie, pulling my duvet over her head.

"Good idea," I agree. "We could be undercover agents and maybe even crack the code."

"What about the wardrobe?"

"What *about* the wardrobe?"

"Shall we use it to hide?"

"Too small," I sigh, "like most of my clothes hanging inside it. BUT, as we're thinking undercover we could tie one end of the duvet on to my raft-bed and the other end to my dressing table and then we could BOTH hide beneath it."

"And pretend we're sitting on the bottom of the sea!"

"Like secret agents in an underwater secret palace with dolphins diving over our heads!"

But it's not as easy as I make it sound and the end of the duvet on the dressing table keeps sliding off and we have to weight it with shoes and books, and we are just arranging pillows for thrones when Mum comes in and asks, "Have you got any washing, Minnie?"

This is get-me-into-a-lather annoying, as it's impossibly hard to be undercover and a secret agent in an underwater secret palace, when your mum comes in and blows your cover. I give her some socks and cross my fingers that now she will leave, but Mum, who is never-walk-under-a-ladder superstitious, looks at my shoes on top of the dressing table and sighs, "Minnie Minx, you know it's unlucky to put shoes on a table."

And I sigh back and say, "But they're not ON a table. They're ON MY DUVET COVER, ON TOP OF MY DUVET, ON TOP OF MY TABLE and so that doesn't count!"

And then Dad shouts, "Where are Spike's new nappies, Audrey?" And Mum sighs, "I'm coming, Malcolm," and disappears on a nappy hunt.

Frankie laughs and says, "Let's make a sign saying Minnie-and-Frankie Utd. DO NOT DISTURB!"

So I sneak into the kitchen and tear the back off a cornflakes' packet and with my glitter pens we doodle:

And I push a hole through the top with a pencil, and tie the sign to my door with a purple hair bobble, and Frankie fetches her violin and together we stare at the secret message...

```
vpmhtsyi;syopmd ejprbrt
upi str/ gpt nromh dp
v;rbrt smf vtsvlomh yjr
vpfr yjrtr od s yep [pimf vpom
pm yp[ pg yjr v;pvl nu
yjr npstf/ hp smf hry oy/
oy od upit DRVTRY SHRMY [toxr/
```

But it doesn't matter how much we stare, the code is still as mind-boggling as ever.

"It's just like double Dutch," groans Frankie. "I'll play my violin and you can do the thinking."

"But Frankie, you're good at languages. You already speak *Spaghetti-Italian*. And you're so good at English that Dad says you speak it better than ME, and I've only lived here all of my life."

"Minnie! I've only lived here all my life too!"

"No, you haven't. I thought you were born in fabulous Milan."

"I was," laughs Frankie, "but I moved to England when I was TWO weeks old, and that was when you were FOUR weeks old, so you only had a twenty-eight day head start!"

"Oh," I mumble, and I'm just wondering how much English you can learn in twenty-eight days, when Mum COMES BACK, and I can tell it's her by her pink-painted toes that are paddling across my coral-painted floor, and clearly Mum has learnt very little English because, despite being written in the HUGEst letters, she has completely ignored our sign.

"Mum," I protest, "do you need glasses?"

"Don't be silly, Minnie. But I thought you might want—"

"What we want ... IS NOT TO BE DISTURBED!"

"You won't be wanting these fish and chips then? And I even got you wooden forks and two sachets of salt and vinegar."

And with a salt 'n' vinegar sense of smell, Wanda trots in behind Mum. But this is OK because Wanda can't read signs... But she can polish off a tray of chips! And so can I. I am stomach-rumbling, totally starving. And fish and chips are a once-in-a-blue-moon extra large treat, as we usually have to eat wholefoods. This doesn't mean swallowing a chicken whole, or not chopping up carrots and stuff, it just means not eating from packets (unless it's a packet of lentils or nuts).

So just in case Mum changes her mind and decides we're having lentils instead, I grab the chips and start to squash them into my mouth and splutter, "I thought you might be a spy, Mum."

"And spies," adds Frankie, nibbling some fish, "are very good at secret codes."

"I might be good if I stand on my head," laughs Mum. "That always helps me think."

"I know!" says Frankie. "If Mrs Piper stands on her head, and I play the violin, then we'll definitely crack the code."

"Maybe," I giggle. "But I'd rather eat chips."

"Me too," grins Mum, stealing one from my polystyrene tray before turning herself upside down. Her hair spreads out like a crinkly blonde halo, and, angelically, she stares at the code.

43

I wonder if it's any easier to solve if you look at it from upside down. But I don't think it is because...

"Perhaps Dad could help," croaks Mum, her voice sounding like a distressed toad on account of her throat being squashed in her neck.

"DAD?!" I protest, with my mouth full. "But Dad's unthinkably NOT very clever."

"Course he is," croaks Mum. "He knows how to build a bathroom cupboard... And ride a motorbike...

And take an engine apart on my carpet."

And all of this is lie-detector true, but I'm not too sure that it makes Dad clever.

"You should never underestimate him," croaks Mum.

"What, never ever ever ever?"

"Absolutely," says Mum. "Though one should NEVER say never."

"You've just said never three times!" I tell her. "And, anyway, I like saying never. It's poetically good at rhyming with Trevor."

"Never, ever kiss a Trevor!" giggles Frankie.

And Mum flips herself the right way up and says, "Sorry, girls, being upside down hasn't cracked the code. But if it's not better upside down, how about trying it back to front?" And then she mumbles, "I'd better be getting back to my salad as it might be getting cold."

Frankie and I gobble what's left of our chips, and race to my mirror to hold up the code. But it's back-to-frontingly hard to read and, not only are the words in a different order, but all the letters are swivelled about and we have to concentrate brain-numbingly hard to swivel them all back. Painstakingly we copy them down, but all they say is:

trbrPje dmpoys; iysthmpv
pd hmorn tpg /rts ipu
rjy hmolvstv fms trbr;v
mopv fmipL pey s do rtrjy rfpv
un lvp;v rjy gp [py mp
/yo yrh fms ph /ftspn rjy
/rx otL YMRHS YRTVRD tipu do yo

45

I am very fed up, but Frankie giggles, "If you just pick out the right letters, you can spell $trevor$ from the top two lines!"

"And kiss Frankie Minelli!" I laugh.

"Where?"

"There! f_m = Frankie Minelli and X = kiss!"

"Yuck," cries Frankie. "I'd never kiss Trevor in a million years!" And then we both collapse in fits of giggles shouting,

"NEVER EVER kiss A TREVOR!"

Jaffa Cakes & dolphins

We sit back down in our Underwater Palace, but Frankie has now got bored with the code and wants to draw a picture of Wanda instead. I'm not bored, but Frankie can't concentrate on anything long. She thinks of ideas, but she is not good at sticking with them. Sticking is more of Trevor's speciality: sticking his finger up his nose and trying to find his walnut-sized brain; sticking chewing gum under my desk, or inside my shoes when we've had PE; sticking his tongue out (especially when covered in yoghurt and pretzels); or sticking his nose in where it isn't wanted (which is really just about anywhere).

Frankie tickles Wanda's ears and says, "It's not fair, Minnie. You're fabaroonily lucky to have a dog. All I've got is hamsters."

"I know," I grin, as I get up to fetch my pencil case and my pad of dolphin paper. (This is not paper made out of dolphins, but is lavender-purple, my best-ever colour, and has dolphins swimming across the top.)

"Haven't you filled that up yet?" says Frankie.

"Not yet. I've gone off it a bit. I used to think it was totally special, but now I try to ignore the dolphins and focus on the purple instead. But anyway, I thought you liked hamsters."

"I thought you liked dolphins!"

Frankie has been clever here because she knows I don't NOT like dolphins, and so now I know she doesn't NOT like hamsters. (Unlike me!) It's just that once they were special and now they are not.

"Mum still thinks I love dolphins," I grumble. "And I don't not L♥VE dolphins, it's just that they're everywhere – even my pillow! Three years ago I wanted a bedroom unlike anyone in the whole universe, and Mum splashed dolphins over every inch, and I totally loved it, but now I feel like I'm almost drowning, and my pillow's faded with bobbly bits.

"And the trouble is that Mum still likes it – only last week she said it had given her an idea to turn Spike's room into a jungle with monkeys and lions and tigers and things. And I don't have the heart to tell her I don't want dolphins any more, and I'd really prefer simple purple. Then I could put posters up and

they wouldn't be destroying Mum's work of art."

"I like your dolphin bedroom," sighs Frankie. "It's fabulously better than my room."

"But your room's just like a Jaffa Cake "

"A Jaffa Cake?!"

"Well it's got fluffy brown carpet and three orange walls, and one white wall behind your bed with zillions of orange circles on it. My mum would think it was chocolate-orange bedroom heaven!"

"But all those circles drive me dotty!"

"I never knew that. Dots are so much cooler than dolphins. I'd love to have a dotty bedroom with purple dots on a lavender wall and ... wait a minute ... that's it!"

"What's it?"

"Purple dots! Though I suppose she'd really rather have Pink."

"Who would?"

"Dot, of course! We could decorate Dot's bedroom with dots! Polka dots for a Polka Dotty! She's still got Wayne's old CHELSEA forever bedroom and I promised her I'd think how to change it. She wants Pink, but plain Pink is boring, so maybe she could have Pink dots! Mum could stencil them if

Uncle Jeff would paint her walls. I'll suggest it when she comes to tea tomorrow."

"Dot is coming to tea TOMORROW?"

"Yes," I sigh. "And, as usual, I'll be left to babysit because Mum's too busy with Spike."

"But I thought you were coming to MY house tomorrow. Nerd has got his friends coming over and you were going to save me."

"Oh!" I squeak. "I totally forgot! I don't know how… Oh Frankie, I'm sorry." And I think of Nero, Frankie's brother, who's fifteen, and ten out of ten drop-dead gorgeous and plays in a band called The Spider Tigers. Secretly, I really like him, but I pretend to Frankie that I absolutely HATE him because Frankie doesn't call him Nero, Frankie calls him NERD! How could I have forgotten I was going to see him? But I can't ask Frankie so all I whimper is, "Sorry, Frankie, I really am."

"Hmmph," humphs Frankie. "Well, if Dot is more important than me, then I'll just be tortured by four teenage boys, playing the drums and electric guitars, and I'll probably be deaf when you next see me on account of their terrible din."

"Of course Dot's not more important," I splutter.

"She's just a cling-on… And I could always try and get out of it."

"Don't bother," grumps Frankie.

And I can't tell her that I WANT to bother, and that secretly I want to see Nero. So I don't say anything, and Frankie glares at me and mumbles, "You probably forgot because you were too busy puzzling Dot's new bedroom."

"I'm really, really sorry," I mumble. And I am so upset because Dot is getting in the way again. And I'm so mad with Uncle Jeff, because it's all his fault for working late EVERY NIGHT and I worry that Dot will never go away and I'll be stuck with her forever. I look at Frankie, who is busy sulking and chewing her hair (which is always a very BIG sulking clue), and she seems to be just as upset as me. So I tear out a sheet of my dolphin paper and say, "For my best-ever friend to draw Wanda on."

"How can I draw without felt-tips?" groans Frankie. "Sorry," I say, and pass her a gel pen that smells of strawberries, and my glitter pens that might be good for a sparkly collar, and my best-ever packet of felt-tips (where even the purple is still working), and try an I-am-your-best-ever-friend smile.

51

But Frankie doesn't smile back and I decide it's best to let her cool down. And, as I'm not in the mood for drawing, I go back to the code.

My idea is this: to use only alternate letters. For example, if you take the alternate letters from...

ASBPCIDKEEF IGSH AI TJAKDLPMONLOEP

then, cloak-and-daggerly, what you are left with is...

SPIKE IS A TADPOLE !!

I try it out on Mr Impey's message, but it just leaves me with...

phsisomepbtpsrgtrmdvrrsftvohjvfyrrdy
ppmvopy[gjvplujnsfhsfro/ydptrtyhm[or

And before I can come up with a better solution, Mum comes in with Violetta Minelli and says Frankie has to go home.

I look at Frankie, who doesn't look at me, and then at Frankie's drawing of Wanda, which is not rubber-fetching bad, but is also not picture-framing good, and I'm just wondering what I should say, as Frankie is not in the bestest of moods, when Mum rescues me with, "Great picture, Frankie! You should pin it on your wall."

"*Magnifico,*" squirms Violetta, who doesn't like anything pinned to her walls, let alone a picture of Wanda that looks a bit like a skateboarding penguin.

"Thank you for having me, Mrs Piper," says Frankie.

"It's been a pleasure," smiles Mum.

But it hasn't for Frankie. She still isn't smiling, and still isn't speaking to me, and, when I secretly whisper, "See you at school," either I'm too good at secret whispering and Frankie hasn't heard me, or she's just ignoring me and still in a sulk.

When Frankie has gone I try to stop worrying that she's not my friend, or worse still, that she'll swap me for a new best friend who hasn't got a cling-on. I watch cartoons with Dad, but after an hour I'm still in a panic and I tell Mum that me and Frankie have fallen out. "Frankie's going to be tortured," I tell her, "and will probably turn deaf on account of Nero playing the drums. And I was supposed to be going to save her by going to her house for tea tomorrow. But now I can't because of cling-on DOT!"

by Frankie

"Why don't you ask Frankie here?" suggests Mum.
"But what about Dot?"
"You can both look after her."
"Hmmm," I grumble, trying to picture Frankie with Dot. "I suppose I can ask. I'll give her a ring."

But I'm a bit nervous that Frankie will still not be speaking to me, so I take a deep breath and try to distract myself by singing the whole of "Three Blind Mice" backwards. (And it is much more difficult than you might think, but it makes you forget nearly everything else.) And then I phone, and thankfully Frankie is speaking to me. But when I ask if she'd like to come to my place tomorrow, and if she's managed to solve the code, she laughs and says, "No way, *Poodle Woodle*..."

And my heart sinks and I am just about to hang up when, "...of course I haven't cracked the code, but YES I'll definitely come to tea!"

"Brilliant," I sigh, "but we'll still have to look after Dot." And now I panic that she'll change her mind. But...

"Oh well. At least Dot is better than Nerd!"

And I cannot agree, but I'm not about to put up a fight and Frankie says she'll see me at school tomorrow. I am so pleased that she's still my friend and, after telling Mum, I quickly phone Gran to ask what she knows about rationing. "Too much, dear," replies Gran, "and I'd rather I didn't, especially now you've reminded me about those stinky dried eggs. But food was rationed and was swapped for coupons that were all written down in a little brown ration book. And we had to queue at the corner shop just to get a knob of butter. And you were only allowed a knob because butter was rationed and you had to eat bread and dripping instead."

"I've never heard of dripping," I tell her, and Gran laughs and says, "It's just melted cow, dear."

And I'm beginning to think that easy-peasy-cheesy lentils might actually be secretly delicious, what with snails and melted cow, when Gran adds, "And of course, you don't know the wonders of tripe," (which turns out to be cow's stomach!), "or the delights of faggots," (which are balls of liver and who knows what else!), when thankfully Mum is shouting, "Bedtime, Minnie!" and I have to say, "Goodnight, Gran," and Gran says, "Goodnight, dear, and thank you for ringing."

THURSDAY AT SCHOOL

Carrot sweets & the art of mind-reading!

I am stomach-churningly worried about school today because I am not even close to cracking the code and I have a sneaky suspicion that Brainiac Jenny will have cracked it and I still don't know my nine times table.

But when I tell Dad this he says, "I haven't got time to crack the code, only my egg to eat with my soldiers, but I CAN tell you an easy way to learn your nine times table."

"But the nine times table could never be easy!"

"Never say never," reminds Mum, as she packs a celery and cream-cheese sandwich into my plastic box with a slice of carrot cake and a tangerine.

"But I will <u>NEVER</u> mathematically <u>EVER</u> be able to learn my nine times table! It's the hardest thing in the whole of the universe… Apart from being nice to a cling-on!"

"But all you need to remember," says Dad, "is that all the answers add up to nine. And this is handy as you're also doing the nine times table!"

"What d'you mean, add up to nine?"

"Simple," grins Dad. "One nine is nine, and the answer is nine, and adds up to nine. Two nines are eighteen, and 18 is 1 and 8, and 1 + 8 make…"

$1 + 8 = 9$ "Nine," I giggle. "But what about ten nines?"

"Ninety!"

Then I blush because even I know my ten times table!

"…And 90 is 9 and 0, and 9 + 0 add up to?"

$3 \times 9 =$ "Nine," I laugh, as I butter my toast.

"Three nines?" shouts Mum.

"Twenty-seven," beams Dad. "And 2 and 7 add up to…"

"Nine!" I holler, catching on. "Four nines?"

"Thirty-six," says Dad. "Five nines?"

"Forty-five! …Dad, you're a genius! Six nines?"

"Fifty-four. Gran taught me this trick. And to make it easy, if the question is seven times nine, take one away from seven and what do you get?"

"Six."

"So the answer starts with six! And six and what makes nine?"

"Three, of course."

  "Correct! 6 + 3. So seven nines are?"

$7 \times 9 = 63$

"63!" I squeal. "And eight nines are... 8 −1 = 7, 7 + 2 = 9, so 7 and 2! Eight nines are seventy-two! Nine nines are ... eighty-one!"

"Hooray," cheers Dad. "My daughter is a genius at her nine times table."

And now I can't wait to go to school, and I race Dad there and Dad wins and puffs, "What kept you?"

"My short porcupine legs," I pant, squatting on the school wall. "And it's all your fault – I got them off you."

"Just like your nine times table trick!"

"Thanks," I tell him, and he jogs backwards, towards Arthurs Way, shouting, "My daughter's a genius at her nine times table!"

And I am so embarrassed that I run into school and pretend that I've never seen him before in my life.

☆   ✶   ☆

Mr Impey is in his cherry-red Thursday tracksuit and after assembly we do our nine times table, and totally miraculously I get it all right! Mr Impey is flabbergasted and gives me a gold star and ten out of ten and says, "Minnie Piper, have you had a brain transplant?"

$^{10}/_{10}$

I tell him Dad's trick and Mr Impey is so impressed that he decides to teach the trick to the class and now even Trevor gets it right. Mr Impey is so pleased that he stands on his hands and walks in a circle saying, "Class Chickenpox, you have just won ten marbles for your marble jar." (We're supposed to be Class Chittenmox after a very ancient, famous teacher, but nobody ever calls us that, even Grumpy Hooper.) And then he jumps the right way up and beams. "Now while you're on a winning streak, has anyone managed to crack the code?"

I look at Jenny, but she just joins in with the rest of us and mumbles, "No, Mr Impey."

I am so relieved, but Mr Impey is not so pleased. "Oh dear," he says. "Then I'd better teach you about World War II and Enigma."

"Wot's an enigma?" hollers Trevor.

"You are," grins Mr Impey. "And it means someone or something that is very mysterious."

Mr Impey writes **ENIGMA** in very big letters on the board, and I prepare to switch off because I hate history and I hate war. But before I can start doodling enigma poems I am enigmally surprised to find I am actually enjoying the lesson, and Mr Impey is telling us that Enigma was a code-making machine invented by the Germans. And I must remember to tell Gran, because it was so clever that it could put a message into code in over a hundred and fifty million, million, million ways!

Mr Impey asks if any of us can write one hundred and fifty million, million, million, and Trevor says he could but his pencil isn't working, and Tiffany says she can, but writes one hundred and fifty million, million, million in words (so happily she can't), and Jenny says she can, and it looks like this...

150,000,000,000,000,000,000!

And brainiacally she gets it right.

"Well done, Jenny," says Mr Impey. "Now hands up who's seen a typewriter? ...Good," he grins, as we all wave our hands. "Now hands up who could draw one on the board?"

Everyone's hand goes down like a shot, apart from Frankie's, who's too busy daydreaming and looking out the window at Year 4 playing rounders.

"Great," says Mr Impey, "up you come then, Frankie." Frankie looks shocked, but goes up anyway, and draws a very wobbly sort of a box with what looks like another box sitting on top of it (but is apparently a sheet of paper).

ENIGMA

And then she draws twenty-six little boxes in three rows inside the bigger box for the keys, so twenty-eight boxes all in all, none of which look anything like a typewriter. Trevor says it looks more like a monster in a hat with twenty-six teeth and no eyes!

But Mr Impey is very pleased and says, "Brilliant, Frankie. This is just what Enigma looked like, except that it had an extra set of twenty-six secret letters that lit up behind the first letters. And perhaps, as Trevor is monstrously clever, he could come and draw them on for us?"

"Nah," says Trevor, "no monster's got that many teeth."

"Ah, but the secret letters weren't square, they were round, and lit up like twenty-six monster eyes!"

"All right then," snorts Trevor, giving in and squashing the eyes between the monster's teeth and its hat. And just to finish off he gives Enigma two ears, and Mr Impey claps. Tiffany moans that he's ruined it, but Jenny points out that the ears could be handles, and actually it  looks quite good. (Trevor is really a very good drawer, but he usually only draws gross things.)

Mr Impey says this is now almost exactly what Enigma looked like, and when you hit a tooth an eye lit up. And Trevor's own eyes light up at this because he's very keen on hitting things.

"And on the teeth," continues Mr Impey, "are one set of letters, and on the eyes are another set of letters, and you might spell CAT on the teeth and get DOG on the eyes, and the eyes light up for only a moment so you have to be quick to see what it says. And then you send the secret message DOG to your friend and they type in DOG on their Enigma and the word CAT comes up! That's how the Germans sent secret messages during the war. And every day they changed the code so that CAT spelled something else."

"My cat can't spell anything!" laughs Jasen.

But Mr Impey ignores him and says, "Although the Germans were really clever, the English code-breakers were even cleverer. They built their own machine, which was the world's first-ever computer, and it was called Colossus because it was so big and wouldn't even have fitted in our classroom. And with the help of Colossus the English cracked lots of the Germans' secret messages. And now..."

"Here comes the bad bit," grumbles Trevor, sticking his pencil into his ear.

"...I'd like you to take it in turns to investigate Enigma or Colossus on the Internet."

"Told you," yawns Trevor, as Mr Impey writes up some websites on the board.

"…And if you're waiting to use a computer," says Mr Impey, "you can draw a picture of the monster Enigma on a piece of paper that Jasen and Abhi will kindly hand out."

One of the good things about Mr Impey is that he lets us use the computers a lot more than Grumpy did because Mr Impey is mad on computers. But the bad thing is that we always have to work in pairs and today I have to work with Tiffany Me-Me and Frankie has to work with Brainiac Jenny.

But Frankie and Jenny are having fun and Frankie is giggling and I am not. When it's our turn Tiffany says, "Me, me, me," and whilst I think enigma thoughts, I happily let her do all the work.

At lunchtime me and Frankie hide behind the pet shed and try to think of something we can do after school that might be fun in spite of Dot.

"How about playing Twister?" I offer.

"Dot's legs are much too short," groans Frankie.

"Then how about playing hide-and-seek? We can both hide really well and Dot'll never find us!"

"Or … we let Dot hide," suggests Frankie, "and then we never bother to find her!"

But I know I could never be that mean. "Mmmm," I mumble. "Maybe not. I'm supposed to be being nice, remember?" And I dip in my lunchbox and my carrot cake has got stickily smashed and looks even more disgusting than it did to begin with. I am just squashing it into a squidgy ball when Trevor spies us and comes to stick his nose in as usual. "Wot's that?" he dribbles, his mouth full of yoghurt.

"A new kind of sweet," I fib. "So new that nobody's tried it and I'M going to be the first. It's guaranteed to be delicious, but you could buy it for 20p."

"Only got 5p."

"That'll do, you can buy a quarter." And I pull off a wodge and mould it into a sticky ball and Trevor swipes it and stuffs it into his yoghurty mouth and then runs off with MY 5p! But I have the last laugh, because I run after him and shout into his sticking-out ears, "That sweet is made out of carrots!"

"Carrots?!" squeals Trevor. "No one ever makes sweets outta carrots."

"My mum does," I tell him. "And my mum made that sweet!" And I know that Trevor hates vegetables, especially carrots, and he promptly turns a cabbagy green and is very nearly sick.

☆   ☆   ☆

After lunch we learn about **BLACKOUTS**, and this doesn't mean we learn about fainting, but putting doubly-thick curtains up to your windows when you live in a war, and turning out your lights teatimely early and then the bombers, who are flying in aeroplanes, cannot see you and just keep flying. And then we learn about evacuation and Trevor says, "I need to evacuate my stomach RIGHT NOW or me and the rest of Class Chickenpox will definitely black out!" And he's still cabbage-green as he looks at me and snarls, "It's your fault, Piper. You an' your mental carrot sweets. JUST YOU WAIT!"

But I cannot wait if I'm going to undo my stupid mistake of telling Trevor the truth of my cake. So I try to backtrack and keep my nerve and say, "Why don't you give me my 5p and I'll tell you what was really in the sweet! Of course it wasn't carrots!"

"Don't need to waste 5p on that. I've learnt the art of mind-reading an' it involves a sharp pin an' your finger!" laughs Trevor.

Fortunately Mr Impey has heard us and sends Trevor to the loos to evacuate, and then stand outside Grumpy's office. I bite my nails and look at Frankie, and Frankie whispers, "Don't worry, Minnie, Trevor's brain's fabaroonily small and much too tiny for mind-reading. In fact he's probably evacuating his only brain cell right this very moment."

Mr Impey is writing the word **EVACUATION** on the board and saying it means lots of children who lived in London during the war had to move to the country because London was dangerous and the country was not. And they had to leave their parents behind, and it was very upsetting and they were totally lonely and sad. And then he tells us that, for tonight's homework, when we go to bed and turn out our lights, we should try and imagine we've been evacuated and see how we feel.

Grumpy Hooper would never say this. Grumpy Hooper would say learn to spell evacuation and when you've learnt it learn it again.

THURSDAY AFTERNOON

 Gobstoppers & trout

After school, Mum meets me and Dot and Frankie. Spike and Wanda are in Spike's buggy and Dot asks if she can push them both, and whilst she pushes she warbles, "How much is that doggy in the window? The one with the waggly tail."

Frankie whispers, "Maybe we should hold a singing contest with Dot?"

"Good thinking," I reply, "except you seem to've forgotten I CAN'T sing."

"Course you can," giggles Frankie. "You're a fabaroony singer – as long as other people are singing loudly with you!"

"I'd be booed off. But you could sing a duet with Dot and I'll get on with the code."

"No way!" whispers Frankie. "I'm not being left with Dot!"

☆   ☆   ☆

When we get home we still haven't decided what to do, so Mum suggests we should be Dot-and-Minnie-and-Frankie Utd. Frankie and I are best-ever friends and I know what she's thinking and she knows what I'm thinking, and what we are thinking is Minnie-and-Frankie Utd is special and, though Dot is having a hard time, she's still a five-year-old cling-on. Mum, who is sometimes telepathic, says, "You could always sit in your Underwater Secret Palace and think up a better idea."

Dot is very keen on this, so whilst she fidgets and "wobbles" her tooth, me and Frankie stretch my duvet from my bed to my dressing table and when we have finished we sit beneath it and try and think of a name.

Frankie suggests, "Minnie-and-Frankie-and-Dotty Ltd."

And I offer, "Minnie-and-Frankie-and-Dot-and-Co."

Dot says, "What's a Co?" and I say, "It is probably Wanda."

But we cannot agree, so I change the subject and ask Frankie what she was searching for on the Internet that was so much fun with Jenny.

"Ballet," giggles Frankie. "Jenny's a wiz on the computer. AND she kept her eye on Mr Impey and gave me a secret signal when he came too close."

"Ballet?" I protest. "And Jenny was your special lookout?"

"I do ballet," sniffs Dot.

"Fabaroony," grins Frankie, "then what you must do is look up www.ballet.org.uk."

"www Dot?" asks Dot. "You look up my name?"

"No!" sighs Frankie.

But to prove I'm as wizzon the computer as Jenny I shout, "YES, ACTUALLY!" For I've suddenly had the best idea... "That's the answer to finding our name... We should be www.minnieandfrankie.co.uk." And I shout the "dots" really loudly.

Frankie thinks this is e-mailingly, mind-numbingly, absolutely brilliant because Dot isn't really in it at all! And she doesn't even suspect a thing! And to celebrate we doodle a brand-new sign...

...and hang it on my bedroom door.

wwwDOTminnie and frankie DOTcoDOTuk

Underwater Secret Palace

DO NOT DISTURB!!

Dot loves it because she thinks she's in it three times, and now she is happy cuddling Wanda (who is also happy as she is the Co).

"I wish I had a Co dog," sniffs Dot.

"Me too," sighs Frankie.

Dot and Frankie don't have dogs, and with this and singing and doing ballet, they are starting to have a lot in common. They also both have other pets – Frankie has her hamsters and Dot has rabbits called Flopsy and Mopsy.

"How are Flopsy and Mopsy?" I ask.

"Not happy," grumbles Dot. "They don't do living on a balcony, and they don't have a garden and dandelions."

"Oh," I sigh, and I wish I hadn't mentioned them because now Dot is sniffly again.

"I like rabbits," says Frankie. "I wish I had rabbits instead of hamsters."

"I like hamsters," says Dot. "Have your hamsters got nice names?"

"*Belissimo*," giggles Frankie. "Gemma and Gemella!"

"Oh," whimpers Dot, who is not so sure these are *belissimo* names until Frankie explains, "Gemma means jewel and Gemella means twin sister."

I explain to Dot that Frankie speaks another language and it's called *Italian*, and Dot says, "My mum speaks another language and it's called France and she says it to me when she rings me at bedtime. *Bon* means good and *bon-bons* mean sweets."

"*Très bien*," says Frankie, showing off.

And I'm not sure if it's because of the singing and ballet and both wanting dogs, but Frankie is suddenly not so grumpy with Dot and tells her, "Gemma is called Gemma because her eyes are like jewels and they *SPARKLE* like stars..." And then, I can't believe what I'm hearing, she adds, "...especially when I say the name DOT!"

"You told Gemma the hamster my name?"

"Course I did," grins Frankie. "I told her you're

five, and a hamster lover and you have curly black hair and a button nose that's covered in freckles and big brown eyes and ... and when I say 'Dot' she squeaks!"

And I don't like to be disbelieving, but I am secretly looking for crossed fingers. But I can't see any, and Dot is smiling and wobbling her tooth and saying, "Where do your hamsters live, Frankie?"

"In their palace," beams Frankie, "which is fabiozo and has indoor wheels and bells and everything, and we all sleep together in my Jaffa Cake bedroom."

"You've got a Jaffa Cake bedroom...? I've got a CHELSEA forever bedroom and Flopsy and Mopsy don't have a palace and have to sleep outside."

"But rabbits like sleeping outside," I protest. "That's what rabbits do, Dot. That's a rabbit's speciality."

"But not on a balcony," whimpers Dot. "They liked my garden a whole lot more."

And then I remember what will cheer her up and I'm about to tell her my plan for her bedroom when...

"Fabaroony!" squeals Frankie. "That's it! Why don't I look after your rabbits, Dot, and YOU look after my hamsters? I've got a garden and grass and everything and you could come and visit!"

Dot and I are astounded at this, and it's totally strange because usually the very last thing that Frankie would want is Dot coming to visit. It is highly suspicious, but I suddenly wonder if it's got a lot to do with Frankie finding a sneaky solution to re-homing her hamsters that once were special and now are not.

But Dot seems happy, and it does seem like a good idea. "We'll have to speak to Uncle Jeff," I say.

Frankie jumps out from under the duvet and says, "Can I borrow your phone, Minnie?"

"What, to speak to Uncle Jeff?"

"No way, *Doodle Noodle*! I need to talk to Dad … about picking me up." And she runs into the hall, and whilst she is gone I tell Dot that Frankie's *Jaffa Cake* bedroom has lots of dots, and how I'd been thinking that maybe dots would be good for her, too.

But Dot thinks I'm dotty and doesn't like the idea at all and sniffs, "I'd rather have *Pink* and pictures of hamsters."

And I'm just wondering if she could have *Pink* hamsters all over her walls when Frankie returns with a smile.

"Could I see them every week?" asks Dot, as Frankie sits back down beside us.

"Who, Dot?"

"Flopsy and Mopsy."

"Sure," grins Frankie, but this time I notice her fingers are crossed. And I'm just trying to whisper, "What are you up to?" when Dad knocks on my bedroom door. He has read our sign and, so as not to disturb us, he has made his own sign which says:

T IS READY! U R NOT!

Frankie and Dot think this is hilarious, and then Dad says, "Did you hear the joke about the skunk?" and Frankie says, "No," and Dad says, "Never mind, it's a real stinker!"

Frankie and Dot are still giggling as we sit at the swinging-manners-teaching table. And now they have even more in common, for they love Dad's joke, and they are both wishing that their tables and dads weren't nearly so boring.

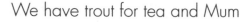

We have trout for tea and Mum has barely put it on the table when Dot sniffs, "I don't do fish, Aunty Audrey." And I have a sneaky feeling Mum knew she'd say this because suspiciously quickly Mum says, "That's OK, Dot, because it isn't fish, it's trout."

Frankie looks at Mum and whispers, "But Mrs Piper, a trout IS a f—" when I just manage to stop her mid-sentence by pinching a buttery lump of potato that she has just covered in tomato ketchup. Frankie looks at me as if I am loopy and says, "Why did you do that, Minnie?"

I glare at her with bulging eyes and whisper, "I can't tell you right now."

"Fine," sulks Frankie, chewing her hair. "Well, as I'm obviously saying the wrong thing I won't say another word – ever, ever, ever!"

And when I say sorry she completely ignores me, and when I offer her extra ketchup she ignores me even more.

After tea, Dad says he has just the thing for trout-eating cousins and feuding friends who aren't speaking, and he goes to the kitchen and returns with a pink stripy paper bag and three *SHINY* gobstoppers. Noisily, we clamour to get one, but... "WAIT!" he teases, waving the bag with his back to Spike. "You can only have them when Spike is in bed and then I can get some peace and quiet."

But Frankie and I were already quiet on account of our NOT talking – and now we're NOT NOT TALKING on account of Dad's sweets! And when I tell Dad this he gets very fed up and says, "I'll never understand girls, Spike, not if I live to be one hundred and nine and fifty-three eighths."

And Frankie does a quick calculation and says, "Excuse me, Mr Piper, but that would make you one hundred and fifteen and five eighths."

And Dad sighs and says, "It's me and you, Spike. Me and you against the world."

Frankie and I run to my bedroom and hide in the Underwater Palace, and Frankie whispers, "I'm sorry I nearly spilt the beans about the trout, Minnie. I get it now. Your mum was being sneaky with Dot."

"It's OK," I tell her. "It's just that Dot's such a fussy eater."

And talk-of-the-devil, Dot arrives and sniffs, "Why are you doing whispering?"

I cross my fingers and say, "We are not doing whispering, Dot. We're just deciding what to do. Would you like your gobstopper?"

"Will it make my tooth come out?"

"No," laughs Frankie, "only toffees do that."

"Oh," sniffs Dot. But we decide to keep the sweets for later and think of what else we can do now. "I do dressing-up and ballet and doing the splits and stroking Wanda," says Dot.

This doesn't sound like fun, so I try to ignore her and say, "How about playing charades, Dot? It's not on your list, but it's totally funny and we get to mime the words we're thinking."

"No thanks. I don't do sharrarz. I only do dressing-up and bending backwards and doing the splits and…"

"…stroking Wanda," sighs Frankie.

"NO!" sniffs Dot. "I also do believing in fairies."

"Fabaroony!" shrieks Frankie. "Why don't we go

looking for TOOTH fairies, then? And if we find one we can let her know about your wobbly tooth, Dot!"

"Oh," sniffs Dot. "But could we do looking for my dad as well, Frankie? I think he's running away like Mum because he keeps on leaving me with Minnie and Gran and I hardly get to see him."

"Uncle Jeff's not running away!" I laugh. "It's just that he has to work late."

"He never used to work late," sniffs Dot. "And if he runs away there'll be only me ... except for my rabbits. And I'll be stuck with CHELSEA FC forever for ever!"

And she starts to cry and to try and cheer her up I pick up my dolphin notebook and pen and say, "Let's go looking for the tooth fairy AND hunt for Uncle Jeff clues! Evidence, Dot, that's what we need. And we'll take the gobstoppers to help us think."

Dot stops crying and I ask Mum if we can pop out and she says, "As long as you stay in Arthurs Way... And don't be long."

"We like you short!" chuckles Dad. "And don't forget to wear your jackets."

"We have to wear our jackets," sniffs Dot, "because we need the pockets for gobstoppers and evidence."

"What EVIDENCE?" demands Dad. "Minnie Minx, what are you up to?"

I can see that Dot is dying to tell him, but not wanting to stir up trouble (because Dad might panic if he thinks his brother is running away, and I'm fairly sure that it isn't true), I cross my fingers and say, "That would be telling, because evidence is confidential, which means it is secret, and not ever to be told to a soul."

And before Dot can spill the beans we set out on our top-secret mission.

THURSDAY EVENING

Bully: chocolaty, Dotty detecting

Block B, Arthurs Way is a little bit like Buckingham Palace. It is not at all glittery and has lots of windows and is ENORMOUSLY wide and has lots of people living

Inside it, and its front garden is made of concrete. But it does not have guards with busby hats or horses

parading up and down and people with cameras waiting for the Queen. Instead, it has boys on bikes and teenagers with drinks cans and stray cats and dustbins.

There are sixty flats in the whole of Block B and they are all joined by a long corridor that starts at the beginning with Flat 1 and goes all the way round three floors and up some stairs, that are made of concrete and are nose-holdingly smelly. Everyone's front door steps on to the corridor, and everyone's back door steps on to a balcony. Once you are in the corridor there are front doors on one side and a wall looking on to the outside on the other.

Block B has got me, Dad, Mum, Spike and Tiffany Me-Me, and Block A has got Gran, Dot, Uncle Jeff, Abhi and Jasen and, very unfortunately, Terrible Trevor.

Not really knowing what clues we are looking for, I try my best to come up with a plan to keep Dot happy. And my plan is this – to start at the top of Block A and work our way down with our eyes peeled and our ears to the ground, and we're just turning into the top-floor corridor, when Frankie hauls us behind a dustbin. Dot is about to whinge in protest, when Frankie puts her finger to her lips and points round the bin at Terrible Trevor, who is pootling our way with a bag of slugs' crash helmets (or snail shells to Dot and Frankie).

"Quiet, Dot," I whisper. "I don't want Trevor to see me right now because he wants to read my mind with a very sharp pin!"

"All right," says Dot, not staying quiet, "but do you think Trevor has EATEN those snails?"

"Of course not," whispers Frankie. "Snails have got to be cooked in garlic and Trevor would never know how to do that."

And we crouch behind the bin, huddled together, and decide now might be a good time to suck on our gobstoppers to keep us quiet as mice.

But the sweets and hiding don't work and Trevor is soon towering over us, looking as thin as a whisker, and taller than ever, which is probably due to his tight jeans finishing peculiarly short of his feet. Thankfully, he seems to have forgotten about reading my mind ... but he hasn't forgotten he's lost his manners and grunts, "Well look who's bin dumped with the rubbish, then! Hey, Piper. You spyin' on me?"

And we're all so nervous we nearly swallow our gobstoppers whole. So we stickily remove them and, whilst Trevor is busy checking his snails, we slip them into our jacket pockets as Dot says, "Why don't you read her mind and find out, Trevor?"

I glare at Dot and suggest she sucks on her gobstopper again before she can say another thing.

"We're just looking..." panics Frankie, sneakily peeking over the outside wall to change the subject and throw Trevor off our scent.

It's then that I notice a tin badge – attached by a pin to Trevor's cap! The badge says bad'n'mad and I wonder if he is going to be bad'n'mad enough to use it to stab my finger and read my mind! But thank finger-tingling goodness, he doesn't appear to have heard Dot's suggestion or remember his threat from this afternoon and I wonder if he did actually evacuate his brain. It's hard to tell, but right now he is following Frankie's gaze over the wall and grunting, "Lookin' for wot, Minelli?"

"Blues," whimpers Dot, obediently sucking her gobstopper again. And she doesn't know that you never ever tell Trevor the truth. It's always best to be ramblingly vague and then he gets lost as you try to explain. But tongue-tyingly thankfully (because of the gobstopper) Dot can only say "blues" and not "clues" and Trevor is easily baffled.

"Blues?" snorts Trevor. "Wot sort of blues?"

But, before Dot can say anything more, I tell him, "We are overly interested in navy blue, but Mr Impey's tracksuit blue is especially, totally, really nice and sky blue is our least favourite, apart from blue rinse which is the colour Gran's friend dyes her hair."

Trevor stares. "You're mental, Piper. An' I know you're lying cuz there's nothing blue behind that bin."

"Wrong!" I tell him. And I snatch at some litter behind the bin and hold up a wrapper of Bubbly Milk Chocolate ... and, thank Chocolate heavens, it's blue!

"By Dab eabs dat chocdate," gabbles Dot, round her gobstopper.

"Wot?" snarls Trevor.

"Her dad eats that Chocolate!" grumbles Frankie.

Trevor yawns and grunts, "Fat-free rubbish. It's just as bad as eatin' lettuce." And then he humphs and plods away gargling, "Blinkin' bonkers Minnie Piper... Absolutely blinkin' bonkers!"

When he has gone Dot trembles, "Is dat wrabber a blue, Binnie?"

And Frankie seems to've forgotten that she and Dot are now "got-so-much-in-common" friends and groans, "Of course the wrapper isn't a clue, Dot. It's only silly chocolate paper."

Bud id mighd lead do finding oub whab by dab's ub do. By dab dikes dat chocolate dods and dods.

And I close my eyes and try to focus on what she is saying, and at last I translate it to, "But it might lead to finding out what my dad is up to. My dad likes that chocolate lots and lots." And surprisingly I have to agree. "Well done, Dot! I don't know what this is going to tell us, but this may be our Number One Uncle Jeff Clue!"

And in my purple dolphin notebook I draw a picture of Bubbly Milk Chocolate.

Bubbly. ⟶ Number One
Clue

And then I write, "Uncle Jeff's favourite chocolate. IS IT HIS?? When did he drop it? Are we on his trail at last? What is he up to????"

Frankie says, "I would have only written chocolate," and Dot mumbles, "Whad shabb we dook for dext, Binnie? ...Oh, helb, Binnie, my dooth hab come oub!"

And she dribbles out her gobstopper and opens her mouth, with a black gaping hole at the front of her teeth, and her tongue is quivering like blue-raspberry jelly, and in the middle of the jelly, like a biscuit crumb, sits Dot's bloody tooth.

I close my eyes to pick it up. I've never touched another tongue before, especially a blue and bloody tongue and, just as I think that I might be sick, I hand Dot her tooth. "Thanks, Minnie," says Dot. "You're my bestest cousin. Shall we call my tooth Number Two Clue?"

Frankie laughs, but I agree to jot it down in my notebook, because all good puzzlers are known to jot. And I take Dot's gobstopper and am just wrapping it in a sheet of my notebook when, who should come back like a very bad smell, but the pungently Terrible Trevor.

Frankie groans, and Dot jumps and drops her tooth and, as it hits the floor, like the throw of a dice, Trevor snorts, "Wot's that?"

"My tooth," sniffs Dot.

"Not any more. Finders keepers!" And he snatches it from under our noses!

"TREVOR!" I shout. "GIVE THAT BACK!"

"Wot's it worth?"

"50p," mumbles Dot. "From the tooth fairy."

"Tooth fairy?" snorts Trevor. "Dotty Daydream believes in tooth fairies!"

"Of course she does," I tell him. "Only an idiot would NOT believe."

"You callin' me an idiot, Piper?"

"That depends."

"Depends on wot?"

"On if you believe in fairies," snaps Frankie.

"Course I don't. Only girls believe in fairies."

"That's because we're cleverer," I tell him.

"Huh?" snorts Trevor.

"How many teeth have you got?" I ask.

"I dunno."

"That's because you're not a girl."

"Twenty," shouts Frankie.

"Exactly," I nod, crossing my fingers in the hope that she's right. "Twenty teeth."

"Don't mean nothin'," grunts Trevor. "An' wot's it got to do with fairies?"

"Money, Trevor. Hard cash. Teeth are worth a lot to fairies."

"50p!" mocks Trevor.

"But not just one 50p. Ten front teeth at 50p, plus ten back teeth at 20p. And all that means that we girls will be..."

"£7.00 richer than you boys," shouts Frankie, as I try to work out the sums. "And that makes US girls fabiozo clever and you, Trevor, fabiozo stupid. Therefore, BELIEVING in fairies IS CLEVER and NOT BELIEVING is NOT."

Dot claps and Trevor is baffled and, after counting his teeth, he departs with brain ache ... and Dot's tooth!

"Stop!" shouts Dot, charging after him. "If you don't believe in fairies, then give me back my tooth."

"No," honks Trevor, "it's worth 50p."

"But the fairy won't come if you don't believe," shouts Dot.

"Well I DO believe."

And just then Abhi and Jasen turn into the corridor. Trevor hasn't seen them, but Frankie has and quick as a flash she shouts, "Believe in what? Tell us and then you can keep the tooth."

"Girls just go on an' on," groans Trevor. "An' all right, I BELIEVE IN FAIRIES."

"YES!" I holler. Abhi and Jasen burst out laughing, and Trevor's face is the perfect picture as he turns to see them run back down the corridor singing, "Trevor believes in fairies, Trevor believes in fairies."

Dot and Frankie are squealing with delight, but this soon turns to tongue-tied terror when Trevor looks like he might EXPLODE. I decide our only hope is a bribe, "I'll swap you a sweet for the tooth," I panic.

"I've 'ad enough of your sweets, Piper."

"Not carrot sweets," I tell him. "These are 100% sugar." And I take my gobstopper from out of my pocket, and wave it in the air to try and tempt him. And he's so greedy, and so mad, that he doesn't see that it's second-hand, or even second-mouthed!

"Double or quits," snorts Trevor, thinking he's clever.

"Of course," I grin. And I unwrap Dot's gobstopper that has now dried with blood-red swirls.

"Marble!" whoops Trevor. "They're the best. Lucky for you I like sweets."

"Very," I giggle. And he tosses Dot's tooth over our heads, hollering, "Never wanted it anyway."

And breathe-again-thankfully he shuffles off, shoving both of our well-sucked gobstoppers into his well-stopped gob.

"We'd better be getting back," sighs Frankie. "We told your mum we wouldn't be long."

"But we've only got one clue." I sigh. "And that doesn't tell us what Uncle Jeff's been up to."

"And we didn't do finding a tooth fairy," sniffs Dot, "and I need one now that I've lost my tooth."

"Don't worry," I tell her, "tooth fairies know when you've lost a tooth. YOU don't have to find them, THEY find you."

"Can we go now?" worries Frankie. "My dad might be waiting."

"And mine," whimpers Dot.

Maybe, I think, as I fetch Dot her tooth. But knowing Uncle Jeff he'll probably be late, and not only will I have no clues to his whereabouts, but I'll have no time to work on the code. YET AGAIN! But I cross my fingers and hope that for once my cling-on is right.

THURSDAY NIGHT

Custard creamily blinkin' crazy!

The finger-crossing amazingly works, because when we get back Uncle Jeff is already there, and Fabio as well. They are both sat at the manners-teaching table having a coffee with Mum and Dad, and it is obvious that they've all been chatting, but as soon as we walk in it goes spookily quiet. I worry they're cross because we've been gone too long, but obviously not as Dad breaks the silence and chuckles, "Hi, girls. Were your ears burning? We've been talking about you!"

"No," sniffs Dot, checking her ears. "But my tooth fell out."

"Uh-oh!" laughs Uncle Jeff. "Your first tooth."

"Did it hurt?" asks Mum.

"Not much, but—"

"She's got it in her pocket," I interrupt, worried that Dot might tell about Trevor's shenanigans, and then Mum will worry and never let me out of the flat again, and Fabio might ban Frankie from visiting. "Why don't you show them your tooth, Dot?"

"OK," sniffs Dot.

"*Bambino!*" wows Fabio, as Dot places her tooth on the table. "That tooth is so tiny it could be a fairy's!"

And Dot grins a toothy smile and plonks herself on her dad's lap. "It IS a fairy's," grins Uncle Jeff, "my Polka Dot fairy's."

And all the parents start talking again and this is nice, but peculiarly odd, as Fabio never stays for coffee, and I don't think he's ever met Uncle Jeff, and it seems as if we're interrupting something, but my brain can't puzzle out what. And then, most peculiarly, Fabio grins and winks at Frankie, and Frankie blushes, and Uncle Jeff winks at Fabio, and Dad winks at Uncle Jeff!

"What's going on?" I laugh. "Why has everyone gone blinking mad?"

"I don't know what you mean," giggles Mum.

"What are you all winking at?"

"Nosy!" grins Dad. "Why don't you have ten minutes in your Underwater Secret Palace?"

"But don't Dot and Frankie have to go home?"

"Not just yet. We won't be long."

"We like you short," laughs Frankie. And I glare at her because Frankie never says things like this. And then she and Dot make off for my room and all the adults laugh.

"There are custard creams in the kitchen, Minnie," says Mum. "Take them to your room to share with the girls. We won't need more than a couple of minutes."

"For what?" I protest.

"Nosy!" shouts Dad again.

And I scream quietly and grab the biscuits and when I get to my bedroom Frankie asks, "Have you got any tissue, Minnie, for wrapping up Dot's tooth?"

"Only loo roll."

"Is it Pink?" asks Dot.

"Peach, I think."

"Do fairies like peach, Frankie?"

"Love it, Dot, it's their third favourite colour after Pink and silver."

"OK then," sniffs Dot. "We'll use that."

And I think I must have been an errand girl in a past life because, after fetching the biscuits, I am now fetching loo roll from the bathroom cupboard, and as I go past the sitting-room the adults are giggling and when I return they are all whispering and huddled together  as if involved in some secret plot. This is highly suspicious and I try and linger to puzzle what they're doing, but Frankie is shouting, "Have you fallen down the loo, Minnie? You're taking ages."

"No," I whisper, as I get back to my room. "I was trying to eavesdrop. All the parents are up to something ... and I think you might know what!"

"Me?" grins Frankie. "Haven't a clue."

"But Fabio winked at you!"

"Oh, he always does that. Especially when he hasn't seen me all day."

"Grown-ups!" I sigh, as I give Dot the tissue. "I'll never understand them."

"No point trying," says Frankie.

"No point trying what?" giggles Dad, as he sneaks up behind me.

"Trying to understand … YOU!" I exclaim.

"Me?" laughs Dad.

"Yes, YOU!"

But before I can quiz him Fabio appears. "Time to go home, Frankie," he grins.

"And you, Polka Dotty," smiles Uncle Jeff.

But Dot's not ready to go just yet and sniffs, "Frankie said I could have her hamsters, Dad, and she could have my rabbits."

Uncle Jeff is suddenly flustered and turns a deeper pink than usual. "But … but it isn't rabbit-swapping day today," he stammers. "Today is Thursday and rabbit-swapping days are never Thursdays."

"What day are they then?" worries Dot.

"That depends."

"On what?"

"Important things, Dot. Very, very important things."

"But … please, Dad," sniffs Dot.

"I'm sorry, Dotty, but the answer is no."

Dot snivels and wraps up her tooth, and Fabio says he must get Frankie home.

"Bye," says Frankie. "See you tomorrow."

"Bye," I sigh.

Then Uncle Jeff and Dot leave too and at last I have time to stare at the code.

```
vpmhtsyi;syopmd ejprbrt
upi str/ gpt nromh dp
v;rbrt smf vtsvlomh yjr
vpfr yjrtr od s yep [pimf vpom
pm yp[ pg yjr v;pvl nu
yjr npstf/ hp smf hry oy/
oy od upit DRVTRY SHRMY [toxr/
```

My brain feels *frazzled* with all that has happened, and I can't think of anything more puzzlingly cryptic than turning A's into C's and B's into D's, moving along an extra letter than I'd tried doing before. But like the *elastic* in my *Princess* pyjamas it doesn't seem to work. So I move along an EXTRA extra letter and turn A's into D's and B's into

E's, but that doesn't work either, and I'm just going mad when I'm saved by the bell...

"Frankie's on the phone," shouts Mum, and I wonder what she wants as she's only been gone for twenty minutes.

"Minnie?" checks Frankie, in a funny whisper.

"Yes," I whisper back. "Why are you whispering? ...YOU HAVEN'T CRACKED THE CODE HAVE YOU?"

"No!" sighs Frankie. "It's because I'm not supposed to be talking to you."

"Why not?"

"If Mum or Dad asks, I never said anything."

"You haven't said anything!"

"That's because I can't. But I can make you think."

"I am thinking. I am thinking you are being peculiar!"

"Sorry, Minnie, but don't you think it's also peculiar that a milkman like your Uncle Jeff should ever, ever work late?"

"I've never really thought about it."

101

"Well you should!" orders Frankie. "You should think about it right now!"

"But I'm trying to solve the code right now."

"This is much more important," says Frankie. "Fabaroonily, much more important."

"Why is it more important?" I ask.

But then I hear Violetta shouting, and Frankie panics, "Got to go..." and in the tiniest whisper, "Remember what I said, Minnie. Go and puzzle it undercover!"

"OK," I whisper back. And Frankie hangs up and I go to my room and climb under my duvet and at first I think she is madly doolally until ... I begin to see that she's probably RIGHT! It is odd that a Dairy Deliverer like Uncle Jeff should ever, ever work late!

I decide to ring Gran, who's always good at solving a mystery, and in thirty seconds I am back at the phone and Gran is saying, "Hello, Minnie. How's the code?"

"Still uncracked and it's got punctuation in all the

wrong places. But that's not why I'm phoning. I was just wondering … why is Uncle Jeff working so late?"

"I … I'm not sure," falters Gran. And this is not like Gran. Gran knows everything!

I decide to press her. "But isn't milk delivered in the mornings?"

"Usually," says Gran.

And just at that moment I think of Dot… "He's not running away, is he?"

"No," laughs Gran.

"Then what is he doing? And will he work late for ever and ever? And what if Aunty Valerie never comes back?"

"What a lot of questions," says Gran. "And of course it won't be for ever, dear. Now how about working backwards on that code of yours? You know, C's into B's and B's into A's."

"But what about Uncle Jeff, Gran?"

"Bed!" orders Mum, who's sneaked up behind me.

"But—"

"Bed!" shouts Dad. "Or you'll turn into a pumpkin!"

"OK," I sigh. "Night, Gran. Sleep tight."

"Goodnight, dear. And thank you for ringing."

I am now certain that something is up. But I don't know what, and as I change into my *Princess* pyjamas I think about Dairy Deliveries and the parents winking and Dot's tooth and tooth fairies and blood-swirled gobstoppers and Terrible Trevor and codes and clues and *Bubbly Milk Chocolate* and ... and it's all too much and I collapse on my raft-bed and go undercover and completely forget about my evacuation homework until Mum comes in and says, "What did you think of my carrot cake?"

"It made Trevor sick."

"That good?" grins Dad, peeping over her shoulder.

"Why were you all winking tonight?"

"Nosy!" chuckles Dad.

"Grr," I sigh. "But why is Uncle Jeff working late?"

"Because..." says Mum, "that's what adults do, Minnie. Dad and I are working late: Dad is working on his motorbike engine and I'm ... doing my yoga."

But being undercover has sharpened my wits. "You've got your painting apron on!" I tell her. "And I bet you're not doing yoga in that!"

"Might be," smiles Mum.

But I know that she isn't, and I guess she's probably painting something for Spike, ready for his jungly safari bedroom. "Is it a tiger or a monkey?" I ask.

"You'll see," smiles Mum, as she turns out my light.

"But why can't you tell me?"

"You'll see," repeats Mum, and I wonder if perhaps she's painting a parrot. If not, she's definitely talking like one.

"UUUUGGGHHHHHH!" I scream. "You're ALL up to something ... I KNOW you are!"

"Sssssshhhh!" whispers Mum. "You'll wake Spike."

"I don't care! I HOPE HE KEEPS YOU AWAKE ALL NIGHT!" And I turn my head, with my face to the pillow, and refuse to look at them for a moment longer.

"Night-night, Minnie," whisper Mum and Dad.

But I don't reply and I close my eyes and count

to a thousand and, when I get to a thousand and one, I dare to look and they've both gone. I drum on my wall and Wanda peeps her head round my door, and this time I don't bother tapping my duvet because I get out of bed and pick her up and snap the door shut and stuff my jacket across the bottom so that the light from the hall disappears. And as if things aren't bad enough already, my no-elastic Princess pyjamas fall down around my ankles!

"I WISH I COULD BE EVACUATED RIGHT NOW!" I scream to Wanda. "And I wouldn't even cry one bit!"

☆   ★   ☆

After ten minutes of lying in the dark, and trying to think myself sad at leaving Mum and Dad, as I'm being evacuated on a train to the country, all I can picture is me shouting, "Good riddance!" as I merrily wave them both goodbye.

Then, being careful not to wake Wanda (who's a useless secret agent, because she's already asleep and I haven't even given her the secret signal), I go undercover and turn on my nightlight and set about cracking Mr Impey's impossible code.

And I don't care if it takes all night, I'm going to stay up until I've done it!

```
vpmhtsyi;syopmd ejprbrt
upi str/ gpt nromh dp
v;rbrt smf vtsvlomh yjr
vpfr yjrtr od s yep [pimf vpom
pm yp[ pg yjr v;pvl nu
yjr npstf/ hp smf hry oy/
oy od upit DRVTRY SHRMY [toxr/
```

I squint and scribble and scribble and squint and all the time I am working backwards, as Gran suggested, but I cannot believe it – it doesn't work! Because...

Uolgsrxh;rxnolcdioqaqstohrsq/fosmqnlg
cou; qaqsrleusruknlgxiquoeq xiqsqncrx
do[ohleuonlol xo[ofxiqu;ou kmtxiqmors
e/gorleqqxnx/nxnctohscqusqxrgqlx[snwq/

...doesn't spell anything!

Exhausted, I try again, in case I've gone wrong, but eons later I still come up with the same answer. I look at my clock and it says ten to twelve! I never, ever stay up this late, except at sleepovers, and I'm so tired I start to feel sick, and after all my efforts, working backwards was not the answer and I was totally sure I'd do it this time. Gran must be slipping. And that's not like Gran. Gran is always totally right!

FRIDAY AT SCHOOL

Dragons & Mrs Bottomley!

I always like Fridays because it's nearly Saturday and Saturdays mean no Trevor. But this Friday is extra special because:

a) Frankie gives me a flag-wavingly snazzy red, white and green *Minellis Deli* bag to replace my BARGAIN BANANAS,

b) the bag contains a fancy sandwich that looks a bit like a squashed French stick stuffed with salami and ham and salad,

c) nobody else has solved the code, and

d) Brainiac Jenny is on the brink of giving up!

But Mr Impey (who's in Friday-black) is not so happy and aims to bribe us into solving the code by juggling four marbles into the air and promising these and six more in the marble pot if we ever finish his homework.

Trevor asks if he can juggle, but having already lost his marbles, he can't keep hold of them for more than a second, and they roll beneath our desks. Mr Impey laughs and moonwalks backwards across the room and as he does he trills, "Think backwards, Chickenpoxers. Think backwards!"

"But I have thought backwards, Mr Impey. And it didn't work and—"

But before I can finish Grumpy Hooper appears and says Mr Impey must go to the office, and that we all have to finish our work on Enigma. I've already finished so I *scribble* a note to Frankie saying:

I think you're right... it is Odd that a Dairy Deliverer like Uncle Jeff should ever ever work late

Frankie takes the note and writes $^{10}/_{10}$ in silver pen and draws what looks like a *Pink* rabbit with wings, but is, I think, supposed to be a fairy. I draw her three purple question marks **???** and *scribble*, "Are you being an enigma?"

"Mop-head!" Frankie scribbles back. "Think *Pink*! Think *Pink* till it drives you dotty."

But I can't think *Pink*, I can only think purple, and I give up and go back to my thoughts that SOMETHING IS DEFINITELY GOING ON!

☆   ☆   ☆

At lunchtime me and Frankie bump into Dot, who is hopscotching all by herself.

"Did the tooth fairy come last night?" we ask.

"No," sniffs Dot. "I put my tooth on my bed and then it was gone. It never got to go under my pillow and I still can't find it so now the tooth fairy will never come."

"Oh," I say, and before I can think of anything else…

"Why don't we visit the hamsters," says Frankie. "That'll cheer you up, Dot."

It won't cheer me up, but I tag along anyway and wait outside the pet shed. But I can tell that Dot is cheering up because I can hear her giggling, and Frankie is laughing that Millicent the hamster has disappeared up Dot's sleeve and reappeared at her neck.

"See!" grins Frankie. "I told you hamsters are fabaroony. Rabbits couldn't do that."

When she comes out I whisper, "You shouldn't say that, Frankie. You should be promoting rabbits not hamsters. Uncle Jeff's never going to agree to the pet swap idea." But Frankie just laughs and whispers, "Remember what your mum says, Minnie, never say NEVER!"

☆   ☆   ☆

After registration me and Frankie meet Dot AGAIN! I feel like she's Velcroed on to my cardie, and she sits by us in the assembly hall where half of the school is working on a collage of George and the Dragon that is going to wind round the school corridor. It's Mr Impey's idea and the dragon is going to have a bendy long body and each of us will draw a small part and we can make it look however we like and then we are going to join the parts and make one ginormous *ENORMOUS* dragon.

Some of the parents have come in to help: not Mum because she works on Fridays, but Trevor's mum is busying about like she might be Picasso reincarnated (and I think she is trying especially hard to make up for Trevor's bad behaviour). Trevor isn't speaking to her, but I ask her if my table could have a jug of water and she scuttles off to fetch one.

Grumpy Hooper comes in for a nose, but I try to ignore him and concentrate on my purple painting. Frankie is painting her bit silver, and Dot, who was daydreaming about her tooth, didn't hear Mr Impey's words, and instead of drawing a bit of a dragon, is drawing the whole thing!

"Dot's away with the fairies," giggles Frankie. "Or at least she will be."

"Nutty as a fruitcake," I giggle back.

"No," says Frankie. "Just away with the fairies!"

"Whatever," I sigh. And then Mr Impey roars like a dragon and instructs us to try ferociously hard to make our paintings flame-breathingly fierce. Dot's already ferocious because she's lost her tooth and draws the angriest dragon Grumpy Hooper has ever seen in his twenty-nine years of teaching.

113

He even holds it up to show us all and says he's going to frame it. Then he mops his brow with his white hanky and asks Mrs Elliott to get the fire extinguisher in case it comes to life. (I'm sure if Trevor's mum wasn't here Trevor would have got the fire extinguisher and sprayed us all just in case.)

The end-of-school bell goes and we go back to our classrooms to collect our things and Mr Impey smiles, "Have fun, Chickenpoxers! Enjoy your weekend, but don't forget to work on that code!"

"Yes, Mr Impey," we chorus, and I say, "Bye, Frankie. And don't forget to ring me tonight."

Frankie winks and says, "As long as I'm not away with the fairies!" And Dot arrives and Frankie dashes out of the school gate with Brainiac Jenny bending her ear. I shout after her, but she doesn't hear me. She's much too busy, giggling with a brainiac, whilst I'm left behind with a cling-on.

FRIDAY AFTER SCHOOL

Kippers & writer's block

Gran and Spike are waiting with Wanda at the school gate. Spike gurgles and Dot kisses him and we both say, "Hello, Gran … hello, Spike … hello, Wanda."

Dot takes hold of Wanda's lead and says, "I've lost my tooth, Gran."

"How grown up," smiles Gran. "Did the tooth fairy come?"

"No," sniffs Dot.

"Oh, dear," worries Gran, taking a peek at Dot's toothy gap. "And the tooth fairies are usually so good at Arthurs Way."

"Are they?" says Dot. "I thought they might not like my flat because it isn't pretty and fairies only like pretty things."

"Nonsense," says Gran. "There are plenty of fairies in Arthurs Way. I've watched them polishing up 50p pieces with a feather duster and fairy dust."

"But I haven't got any Pink," worries Dot. "And my walls say CHELSEA FC forever and the tooth fairy probably thinks I'm a boy ... and boys are not so fond of fairies."

"I shouldn't worry about that," grins Gran. "Why not make a wish for something Pink?" And, either she has something stuck in her eye, or she is secretly winking at Spike. Whatever it is, she is certainly acting suspiciously strangely – just like Frankie a few minutes ago ... and just like Mum and Dad and Uncle Jeff and Fabio last night ... and just like Uncle Jeff every night!

I can usually always count on Gran, but right now I'm not so sure ... and I decide I need to go undercover to puzzle what's ENIGMALLY going on!

☆   ⋆   ☆

When we get back to Gran's flat I ask, "Have you got a tablecloth, Gran? Dot and I have puzzling to do and, as you say, it is always best to puzzle undercover."

"Ohhhhh?" flushes Gran, a little suspiciously. "What kind of puzzling, dear?"

And I get a very strong feeling that Gran is doing some puzzling herself and beginning to wonder what I might be up to. But not wanting to give my game away, I simply tell her, "My secret code homework, of course!"

"Of course," smiles Gran. "Follow me." And she takes me and Dot into the kitchen and puts her second biggest tablecloth over the table, and it hangs all the way down on two of the sides, but is a little bit short on the others. And then she switches on her tiny telly in the corner of the kitchen, with the volume turned down because Spike and Wanda are both asleep. But it doesn't matter that she can only lip-read because Spellbound is on and she can still see the anagrams and, more importantly, Johnny Sprightly.

"Is Uncle Jeff coming for tea as well?" I ask, as me and Dot hide under the table.

"No dear, he's working late."

I grab my notebook from my *Minelli's Deli* bag and quickly scribble "FRIDAY: Uncle Jett working late again!" And then I signal to Dot to stay snail-squeakingly quiet and say, "Dairy Deliveries seem especially busy at the moment, Gran."

"Do they, dear?" cheeps Gran, chopping up potatoes with one eye on Johnny Sprightly. And then she shouts "RUBBISH!" and Dot and I look out of the other side of the table to see if Spike has woken up. But he's still dreamily in the land of nod, and Gran whispers, "Sorry, dears, I just got a seven-letter anagram."

"What was it?" I ask.

"RUBBISH!" laughs Gran "R. U. B. B. I. S. H. And that silly woman only got rubber."

"How about RUBBISHER?" I beam. "That would be a NINE-letter word!"

"Very good, dear!" says Gran. "Are you doing as well with the code?"

"No, not really. It's too hard, and your backwards clue didn't work."

"That's a pity," says Gran. And I peep my head out from under the tablecloth and ask if she has any more ideas. "As a matter of fact I do," she smiles, "and it concerns Dotty's missing tooth!"

"It does?" squeals Dot, bursting out from under the table to join us.

"Yes," says Gran. "Minnie could write you and the tooth fairy a poem, Dot. Tooth fairies are fond of poetry, especially the ones in Arthurs Way. They set them to music, and while they're out collecting teeth, they dance about our bedrooms."

"They do?" squeals Dot.

"Of course," says Gran.

"Hooray!" cheers Dot. "Write me a poem, Minnie!"

"OK, OK ... but what shall I say?"

"Is that it?" laughs Gran. And Dot looks worried until I reassure her that that isn't it, and I stare at my dolphin notepad and think.

I try...

Tooth fairy, tooth fairy, where have you been?
Have you been up to London to visit the Queen
Instead of Arthurs Way and Dot?
Did you lose your way or what?

"It's a little bit accusing, dear," says Gran. "You need to be at your most politest if you're going to appeal to fairies."

But my next poem is worse than ever...

Dotty needs Some cheering up
One way or another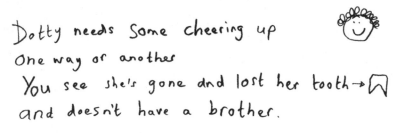
You see she's gone and lost her tooth→
and doesn't have a brother.

"I don't like brothers," sniffs Dot.
"You like Spike!"
"He's not my brother."
"OK, but I can't think of anything else at the moment, Dot."
Gran says, "You've got writer's block, dear, but kippers are a cure."

"That's lucky!" cheers Dot. "We've got kippers for tea!" And despite Dot not "doing fish" when the meal arrives she gobbles it down faster than me and, by the time our plates are empty, I spookily, actually do have my poem!

"THE KIPPERS WORKED!" I squeal. "I've got it, Dot!"

"Told you!" smiles Gran, as I scribble down my poem. And while I doodle she feeds Spike spoonfuls of peas, singing, "Here comes a big green motorbike, open up the garage door."

Dear ~~to~~ Tooth Fairy,

Dotty needs some cheering up
One way or another
You see she's gone and lost her tooth →
And misses her nice mother
Aunty Val has lost her job
And disappeared to France
And poor old Dotty's very sad
And needs more shoes for dance
Dot's very good at Ballet
And has total BENDy joints
She can do the Splits and everything
And would like to have some pointes

P.S. Pointes are what ballerinas wear to do their pirouetting and just what Dotty will need very, very soon.

Thank you very, very much
We believe in you {lots} and {lots}

Yours very politely, and hopefully
Minnie and Dotty Piper
x x x x x

"How did you know I wanted pointes?" gasps Dot.

"Bestest cousins know these things. But you won't be able to wear them just yet, Dot. You'll have to wait till you're big like Frankie."

"But I could do just looking at them," sniffs Dot, "and hang them up by the side of my bed, and then I might have dancing dreams."

"What a good idea," says Gran. And she lifts Dot on to her knee and gives her a cuddle with Spike. "And I know you're missing your mum, Dot, but I know she's always thinking of you, because she told me in a letter."

"She did?" cheers Dot. "Can I write a letter to Mum?"

"Of course," says Gran. "Minnie will help, won't you, dear?" And she turns to me and grins. "Your fairy poem is brilliant, dear. I knew those kippers would be just the thing."

"I love fish!" beams Dot. "I'm going to eat it lots and lots!"

FRIDAY AFTER SCHOOL

Gulping like a goldfish

Before I have chance to start on the letter, Uncle Jeff pops his head round the door and hoots, "Surprise, surprise, Polka Dotty!"

"Dad!" squeals Dot, as she rushes towards him.

"Well close your eyes then, Dot. You can't have a surprise with your eyes wide open!"

"But what is it?"

"You'll see. Hold your hands out and keep as still as a statue."

Dot keeps as still as she can (but it isn't exactly like a statue), and into her hands Uncle Jeff presses the tiniest present I have ever seen. It is all wrapped up in Pink paper and tied with the teensiest, weensiest bow that looks as if it was tied by a fairy.

"Open!" beams Uncle Jeff, and Dot peeps and looks at her present, and pulls at the ribbon and tugs at the paper and there, inside, snuggled up in cotton wool, is none other than...

"MY TOOTH!" squeals Dot. "You've found my tooth! But where did you find it?"

"Under your bed," laughs Uncle Jeff, "a little to the right of a spider's leg and just beneath a piece of peach tissue."

Dot squeals with delight. "That's the tissue I wrapped the tooth in! Thanks, Dad. Aren't you working late tonight?"

"Not tonight. I thought, as a treat, and as it's Friday, you might like me back early."

"I do!" squeals Dot. "But we can't go yet. Minnie's helping me write a letter to Mum."

"Oh," says Uncle Jeff. "Then ... then why doesn't Minnie come home with us? ...Perhaps she could even sleep over?"

"YES, PLEASE!" screams Dotty.

And I try to smile, but really I've seen so much of Dot that I think I'm going dotty myself. And I really want to work on the code, and Frankie is supposed to be going to ring me. But Dot is so happy, and telling Uncle Jeff I'm her bestest cousin, that I feel wicked-cousin bad and have a spooky-sneaky-secret feeling that I'm probably going to say yes.

"Lovely," says Uncle Jeff, when I find myself nodding.

"But I'll need to run home to fetch my things."

"Of course, dear," says Gran.

And my heart sinks as Uncle Jeff helps me and Spike into the lift, which is cheesy-feet smelly, and worse than the stairs. And, I'm so cross that I didn't say NO, and I know I'm supposed to be trying to be nice, but right now I am trying very, very hard to put off going back to Dot's. And as slow as a snail I drag my feet and Spike and Wanda across the garden and into the lift, but when we reach the third floor I am still in a bad mood. "Hi, Mum…" I sulk. "Hi, Dad…"

"Minnie Minx?" says Dad. "What are you doing here? I thought you were sleeping at Dot's tonight?"

"Fancy thinking that!" winks Mum.

Dad looks puzzled and then winks back.

"STOP!" I shout. "Why are you two winking again? And come to think of it, how did you know I was sleeping at Dot's? Uncle Jeff has only just asked me, and he made it sound as though it wasn't planned…"

"It wasn't," says Dad.

126

"It was spur-of-the-moment, off-the-cuff, and—"

"Then how did you know?"

"I … I didn't," splutters Dad. "But—"

"That's nice," interrupts Mum. "Being invited to stay with Dot."

"I'm her bestest cousin and I'm trying to be nice, but don't change the subject! Something's going on and you're talking in riddles and even Gran is acting strangely. And Frankie! …And how did you know about me sleeping over?"

"Because," mumbles Mum. And she scratches her head and screws up her nose and grins. "Oh, yes, I know – Uncle Jeff told me he'd found Dot's tooth."

"So?"

"Well… Dad and I … we were just thinking, weren't we, Malcolm?"

Dad smiles, but says nothing.

"What were you thinking?"

"That … that Uncle Jeff might be nervous about Dot losing it again … and that he might think it would all go OK this time if you were there. So you'd better go… I expect Dot's excited."

"Mmmmm," I grunt, "but I'd better get some Dot-free time after this as I'm TRYING TO SOLVE A CODE!" And I grab my nightie, and lose my school uniform for my funky caterpillars and my purple cord skirt and a new top that Mum's just bought me (which surprisingly fits and is lilac with a purple heart and long purple sleeves). And for once I am pleased with how I look and I can't wait to show Frankie. And this reminds me she was going to phone. "Has Frankie called?" I shout to Mum.

"Don't think so," says Mum.

So I run to the phone and punch in her number and it's Nero who answers with, "Hi, Minnie," and I gulp like a goldfish and fumble, "Can I speak to Frankie, please?"

"Sorry, Minnie, she's not here. She said something about seeing a new friend."

"Oh," I mumble. "Th-th-thanks, Nero." And I put down the phone and my mouth dries up in a dizzying panic. My best-ever friend has found someone else. And she must be special because she's gone to see her instead of ringing me. And

Frankie hasn't told me about her, and secret friends are always special. And I picture myself just hours earlier, calling after her, but she doesn't hear me. She's too busy giggling with Brainiac Jenny. And it's all Dot's fault and I thought this might happen. Who wants to be friends with the friend of a cling-on?

"Everything all right, Minnie?" asks Mum.

I shrug my shoulders and slump on the sofa.

"How's Frankie then?"

"She's out at a friend's."

"Uh-oh," laughs Dad, winking at Mum. And Mum nudges him and they both start laughing.

"It's not funny!" I tell them. "And stop winking!" And I think I might cry, so before I do, I go to the door mumbling, "Bye then, see you tomorrow."

And I run back down the forty-two steps, with my nightie and toothbrush in my bag, and all I can think of is Frankie's new friend. But before I can work out who it is I am outside Dot's flat, which is Flat 13 and unlucky for some.

FRIDAY NIGHT

Bon-bon surprises!

I decide to push Frankie out of my head – if she's having fun with a new friend, then maybe I should too. I try and imagine that Dot is my friend and as we go off to her football bedroom, I am about to say that maybe her room wouldn't be so bad if she changed her name from Dot to Chelsea, when Dot exclaims, "My bed has grown!"

And it certainly has, for there, squashed into Dot's tiny bedroom, is the most **HUMUNGOUS** bed.

"Oh," sniffs Dot. "When Dad said I could have a new bed I didn't think it would be like this. Now there's no room for doing ballet, and I'll never learn to pirouette."

"But it does make the bounciest trampoline," I tell her, as I jump on top of the squishy mattress.

"Oh," sniffs Dot. But as she climbs up to try it the doorbell rings and Uncle Jeff shouts, "Can you get that, Dotty?"

Dot looks anxious, so I tell her I'll get it. And I jump off the bed and Dot comes with me like my cling-on shadow, and there, to our surprise, is none other than Frankie! Most of her is hidden behind an ENORMOUS package draped with a cloth, but it is definitely Frankie because at her feet is the best-ever bag with shiny purple and lilac hearts which is something only Frankie could own. I am lost for words as Frankie giggles, "Well aren't you going to let me in?"

"Course we are," nods Uncle Jeff. "Come on, Frankie. I'll take that." And he grabs the mysterious cloth-covered package, as if he's been expecting it.

Frankie picks up her bag and steps inside, and we all traipse into the lounge, but I'm not exactly pleased to see her because she's either on her way to, or on her way back from, seeing her special new friend. And I'm stuck puzzling, do I behave like her best-ever friend, or like her best-ever friend that has now been dumped?

But Frankie isn't interested in me. Frankie is cheeping like a budgie to Dot. "Well," she giggles, as Uncle Jeff puts the package on the table, "welcome to your new pets, Dot!" And she pulls off the cover, like a magician's assistant, and *magically* reveals ... Gemma and Gemella!

Dot and I are spookily stunned. Uncle Jeff said no to the pet swap, but here he is as calm as a kipper... Unlike me. My knees turn to jelly as I notice the hamsters' scaly feet, and I step back as Frankie puts her head to the cage and says, "Gemma and Gemella, I would like to introduce to you, your fabaroony new owner ... Dotty Piper!"

"Are they really for me?" exclaims Dot.

"Really," laughs Frankie.

Dot looks at her dad to be doubly sure, and Uncle Jeff grins and nods his head. Dot claps and one of the hamsters squeezes into a pipe that curls all the way from the top floor to the bedding at the bottom. Dot is flabbergasted as the hamster shoots like a bullet down the tube. "That's Gemella," giggles Frankie. "She's the one with the black ears."

132

Dot squeaks, "I love black ears!" and almost spins a pirouette as Uncle Jeff says, "Well, Polka Dotty, aren't you going to show them your room?"

"Oh," sniffs Dot, "but there's not much room now I've got a new bed." But she goes to her bedroom and Frankie follows with the cage and hamsters as I hang back as far as I can. My mouth has dried up all over again and I am trying very, very hard not to look at the hamsters' feet and to find a moment to ask Frankie why she didn't tell me she was coming here tonight, and why she didn't ring me, and, most importantly, who's her best friend. But all I can hear is Uncle Jeff saying, "Hey, I don't want them in MY room! They're your pets, not mine."

"But this is my room," sighs Dot, puzzled.

"No it's not," laughs Uncle Jeff. "That's MY room. I've always fancied football curtains. Since when have you been a CHELSEA fan?" And most peculiarly he is winking madly as Frankie giggles, and I am absolutely relieved Violetta isn't here or she'd probably, definitely think we were totally crazy and never let Frankie see me again.

"Oh," sniffs Dot. "But where will me and the hamsters sleep?"

"In there of course," grins Uncle Jeff, and nods to the room that used to be his.

And anxiously Dot opens the door, and me and Frankie follow her in and there ... like Dotty's dream come true, is the pinkest, fairyest bedroom ever!

Gemma and Gemella's Arthur Way Palace

It has **Pink** walls and a **Pink** carpet with a fluffy rug and **Pink** curtains and two **Pink** cushions with fairy wings, and a fairy duvet and a fairy pillow all piled on a fairy bed and…

"**WOW!**" squeals Dot. "Is this all for me?"

"And Gemma and Gemella!" smiles Uncle Jeff. "I've left them a space right THERE!" And he points to a spot on top of a table, and above the table is a sign saying:

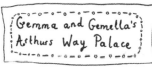

Gemma and Gemella's
Arthurs Way Palace

And above that is a fairy picture, and the fairy has a sparkling wand that is covered in glitter, and the picture is signed (totally suspiciously) *Audrey Piper* ! I never knew Mum had painted this! And then I remember last night, when she came to my room in her painting apron … and I'd thought she was painting a tiger for Spike!

Uncle Jeff lifts the hamsters into their new space and says, "Well, Polka Dotty, what do you think?"

"It's so **SPARKLY**!" squeals Dot, as she does the splits in front of the hamsters.

I'm almost speechless, but I manage to splutter,

"SO THAT'S WHAT YOU'VE BEEN DOING, UNCLE JEFF! YOU'VE BEEN DOING DOT'S BEDROOM!"

"For the past ten nights," laughs Uncle Jeff. "And I NEVER want to work late again!" And then he adds, "Did you find your special present, Dot? It's hidden under your bed."

"Another present?" squeals Dot. "That's four in one day. My tooth, my hamsters, my room and..."

"Fantastico!" beams Frankie. "Fancy having all these surprises. Didn't you know about any of them?"

"No," giggles Dot, diving beneath her fairy bed.

"But I think you did," I whisper to Frankie, "you don't seem to be totally surprised."

But Frankie isn't listening to me because Dot has appeared from under her bed, with the cutest, Pinkest, prettiest present that any of us have EVER seen! It is all wrapped up in candyfloss tissue and tied with a bow of silver ribbons that EXPLODE into glittery, curly springs.

"Open it!" squeak Frankie, me and the hamsters!

"It's not even my birthday," sighs Dot, as she tugs at the paper. And we all gather round as the ribbons fall away and there, inside the glitter and paper, is an even glitterier Pink sparkly dress.

"A fairy dress!" squeals Dot, delighted.

"A French fairy dress," grins Uncle Jeff. "Sent special delivery all the way from France."

And attached to the dress is a tiny card that says,

> Dear Polka Dotty Fairy, Hope you like it. I am thinking about you lots and lots and lots and lots. Do a special dance for me and Dad will take your photo and I will put it by the side of my bed and then I can see you every night.
> Lots of love and kisses, Mum xxxxxxxxxx

"It's from Mum!" shrieks Dot, and she is so happy and giddily dizzy from pirouetting, and she puts on the dress and Uncle Jeff fetches his camera and Dotty pliés and shouts, "THANKS, MUM!" as if her voice might be reaching France. And Uncle Jeff says, "There's more yet, Dotty. Mum has sent you some French food for your first-ever sleepover party."

"Not snails?" gasps Dot.

"No!" laughs Uncle Jeff. "Nice things like chocolates and bon-bons, so you can all have a chocolaty midnight feast."

137

But the chocolates don't last another hour, let alone till the strike of midnight. But they do help Dot write a poem to her mum.

Dear Mum,
I love my room, It is not blue
I love it pink and I love you
xx xxxx Dot xxxxx

And it's actually quite good for a five-year-old cling-on, except she's forgotten to mention her fairy dress.

"Oh," sniffs Dot, when I point it out. "I forgot about that." And she carefully adds,

And I especially love my fairy dress
and I am wearing it Now and I am
always going to be wearing it and I
am putting your card by the side
of my New fairy bed and my tooth
has come out and I have hamsters
Called Gemma and Gemella
xxxxx xxxxx txXxxxxx

And when she has finished she wriggles excitedly in her new bed as Frankie and me put our nighties on and try to get comfy on the floor. I am very nervous of sleeping with the hamsters, but it turns out OK because typically, Frankie arranges herself in a prime position where she can sleep by her pets and is still able to see Dot. I am squashed between Frankie and a wall, but it suits me fine, as I have no desire to see either Dot or the hamsters.

I listen to Frankie talking to Dot, and wonder if she's being polite and paying attention to the hostess of the party, or if Dot's an excuse so she doesn't have to talk to me. I try not to worry as we play "I went to market and in my basket I put..." but I am so nervous about losing Frankie as my best-ever friend that I keep on getting it wrong. But after a bit Dot and Frankie start to get tired and Uncle Jeff says it's time to sleep.

"And don't forget about your tooth, Polka Dotty."

"And my poem!" sniffs Dot. "Minnie wrote it for the tooth fairy."

"You didn't tell me," whispers Frankie.

"You weren't in to tell," I whisper. "You were too busy with your new best friend!"

"But—"

"Splendid," booms Uncle Jeff. "The fairy's in for a treat tonight."

And, as if it was made from crystal glass, as fragile as the tissue that wrapped her dress, Dot takes her tooth, and places it on top of the poem, on top of her sheet, and beneath her fairy pillow. And with that she is suddenly fast asleep and twitching like her hamsters.

I count to a hundred and, when I'm sure she's still asleep, I pluck up the courage to talk to Frankie. I want to ask if we're still friends, and who's her new friend, and my stomach is turning somersaults, and I can't wait a moment longer so I sing the first line of Three Blind Mice backwards and whisper, "Frankie, I thought you were going to phone me tonight. I phoned you, but Nero answered and said you were seeing a new friend. It isn't Brainiac Jenny, is it? You know she's a terrible swot."

But Frankie doesn't hear me. She's too busy snoring in her dark-green sleeping bag, and is out for the count like Dot.

"Great," I grumble. "Now I still don't know if we're friends."

"Everything all right, girls?" whispers Uncle Jeff, as he peeps his head round the door. I pretend to be asleep and he turns out the light and disappears. And then I just lie there, missing Wanda, and miserable and alone with my thoughts, and I wonder if this is what evacuees felt like when they were evacuated to the country. I feel like I've lost my best-ever friend, and all I want is to be tucked up at home on my raft-bed with my stupid dolphins and bobbly pillow.

SATURDAY MORNING

Trixibella & ribbon biscuits

Frankie and I wake to a frantic Dotty who is dizzy with excitement, shouting, "She's been, she's been! The fairy's been! And guess what? She's left me a pound. A whole pound! Gran was right. Fairies do like poems, Minnie, especially a fairy at Arthurs Way. And she's even written ME a poem!"

"Fabaroony," yawns Frankie. "What does it say, Dot?"

"I'm not sure. Her writing's fairy small and some of the words are a bit long."

"I'll read it," I offer, as I rub my eyes and try to focus. And Dot hands me a sheet of pink paper, and there, in the minutest tiny silver writing, is Dotty's fairy poem.

Dear Polka Dotty Fairy,

I'd like to be a dancer,
but I'm really not that good,
I need a room to practise in
and I wondered if I could
From time to time join in with you,
in your dancer's room so pink?
I'd hide behind your curtains, and take lessons.
What d'you think?
I'd really like to learn the splits
and spin upon my toes
And be as good as other fairies
in our Fairy Magic Shows

In secret I'll be watching
and learn everything you do.
And together we can pirouette
in a fairy dance for two.

With very best wishes and a sprinkling of fairy dust ☆

Triscibella Fairy

x x x x x x x x x x x

" WOW! " sigh Dot and Frankie and me, as I hand the letter back to Dot. Uncle Jeff comes to see what all the noise is about and laughs, "The fairy's been then, Polka Dotty?"

"Yes!" squeals Dot. "And she left me a pound and a fairy poem!"

"Goodness me! All that for a Polka Dot fairy? You'd better have some breakfast to calm you down. What would you like? Jam and toast or ... toast and jam?"

"Toast and jam!" squeals Dot. "And I'll make it!"

"OK, but we don't want fairy portions, you know."

But Dot isn't listening. She's off to the toaster in her fairy dress clutching her fairy poem.

"Well I'm glad that's over," laughs Uncle Jeff, as we eat our toast and jam in the kitchen. "Keeping secrets is hard work. I seem to've been plotting this for ever ... with Uncle Malcolm, who made the bed, and Aunty Audrey, who made the curtains and..."

"Mum and Dad?" I protest.

But Uncle Jeff isn't listening. "...AND," he grins, to a beaming Dot, "most importantly your mum has been ringing me every night, telling me how to arrange your room."

"Mum told you where to put everything?"

"Well you know how bossy your mum can get! Even being in France can't stop her!" And then he laughs. "You'd better phone her to tell her all about it."

"*Oui!*" shrieks Dot. "I'll phone her now!"

"Not right now. First we must deliver the rabbits to Frankie's."

"Oh," sniffs Dot.

"If that's all right?" worries Uncle Jeff.

"Will you give my rabbits cuddles, Frankie?"

"Of course," says Frankie. "Fabaroony cuddles!"

"Then I'm sure," sniffs Dot.

☆ ☆ ☆

I am still desperate to talk to Frankie, but now there is so much going on and, while Uncle Jeff fetches Flopsy and Mopsy, Frankie and I get changed. Dot stays in her fairy dress, and refuses ever to take it off, and Frankie packs her purple bag with the lilac hearts and grins, "Your top goes perfectly with my bag, Minnie."

"You could borrow it if you like," I mumble. "It's actually the right size for once."

145

"Thanks," giggles Frankie, "but it might be better if I give YOU the bag! You can't have *Minelli's Deli* forever!"

And she unpacks it there and then and tosses it in my direction. And I can't believe I am upgrading from *BARGAIN BANANAS* to *Minelli's Deli* to the dreamiest bag in the whole of the universe! And it certainly seems as if she's still my friend but I only wish Dot wasn't in the way, so I could actually get a chance to ask.

☆　　　　★　　　　☆

Frankie doesn't live in Arthurs Way. The Minellis don't live in anyone's way. They live in the *HUGE*ST house you have ever seen, and when we arrive they are waiting to greet us.

"Stink-bomb!" squeals Frankie, as she pushes past Nero and into the kitchen.

Fabio is waiting with some Italian biscuits (and they are nothing at all like custard creams and are shaped like ribbons and tied into bows). He has dusted them with icing sugar that he says is fairy dust especially for fairies like "*bella* Dotty". And then we have a drink of freshly squeezed oranges, in very tall glasses with twisty straws, and Uncle Jeff has a cup of coffee that is so small it is gone in a swig and Fabio has to make him another.

"*Morsicano?*" worries Violetta, as Flopsy and Mopsy nuzzle at her feet.

"Course they don't bite," laughs Frankie. "They're cute."

"Cute," I echo, looking at Nero.

But suddenly the dreamy Nero is speaking. "D'you want to see Flopsy and Mopsy's new hutch, Dot? Minnie's dad has built them a new one."

"He has?" I exclaim, jumping out of my stupor. But no one is listening and everyone is following Nero outside. And there, in Frankie's grassy garden ... is

Minnie Piper

the fanciest, most *Splendidest* rabbit hutch ever! It's a bit like a palace, but…

"It's not finished yet!" grins Nero, as he disappears into the garage and comes back with a rabbit run.

"Nero's so strong," I accidentally whisper to Frankie, as he places the run in front of the hutch.

"Only in the odour department!" says Frankie.

And I quickly laugh to extinguish my thoughts and gulp, "Did my dad really build that?"

"Course," says Frankie. "He's fabiozo clever as well as funny."

"YOU ARE JOKING? My dad is definitely, totally NOT clever. And neither is he funny."

"I think he's funny," offers Nero.

"Well sometimes he can be," I blush. And quickly I eat my words, and am now so flustered that I turn my attention to Flopsy and Mopsy, who are hopping happily in their new palace.

"And now I need to return Dot to her fairy palace," grins Uncle Jeff.

"Already?" sighs Dot.

"Don't want your hamsters to be lonely," grins Frankie.

"And..." says Fabio, "...I'll need to give you some ribbon biscuits. You must eat them when you're talking to Gemma and Gemella. They like the smell of ribbon biscuits and I shall have to bake you some every week."

"Thanks!" beams Dot, and she does the splits as an extra thank you and everyone claps, including Nero.

I follow Uncle Jeff to his car, and I am just wondering if I am leaving Frankie's for the last time (because if she now has a new friend she might not want me back), when she says, "You could stay if you like, Minnie. I've checked with your mum and she says it's OK... That's if you want to."

"But what about your new friend?"

"What new fr—?" laughs Frankie.

But she is interrupted by Uncle Jeff. "You staying here, Minnie? Well then I'd better take this moment to thank you girls. I couldn't have done this without you, you know."

"But I didn't do anything and..."

...And Uncle Jeff doesn't hear me — he and Dot are waving goodbye and in the blink of an eye they're gone.

SATURDAY AT FRANKIE'S

Extra large confessions

"BUT I TOTALLY, REALLY DIDN'T DO ANYTHING!
…And it seems like I was the only one, apart from
Dot, who didn't know what was going on!"

"True," laughs Frankie, as ten seconds later
we sprawl on beanbags in her *Jaffa Cake*
bedroom. "But YOU got to play the
fabaroony cousin … and I had to play
the wicked witch who wasn't
allowed to say a word."

HEE
HEE
HEE!

"SO YOU DID KNOW!"

"Of course I knew, but—"

"Did your tongue get tangled so you
couldn't tell me?"

"Sworn to secrecy," whispers Frankie. "But I
have been trying to drop you hints."

"Invisible hints?"

"Dairy Deliverer working late kind of hints … and
my drawing of a fairy *Pink* rabbit … and telling you
to think *Pink* … AND that Dot was away with the
fairies … and that I might be too!"

"But why didn't you just TELL me?"

"I couldn't," sighs Frankie. "Mum and Dad were really strict and threatened me with not seeing you. I had to cross my heart and promise to be grounded for a whole month if I so much as breathed a word."

"But how did your dad know?"

"On Thursday night, when I borrowed your phone, I asked him if I could swap my hamsters, and he spoke to your mum, and she thought it was a good idea as Dot's flat isn't great for rabbits. That's what they were all talking about when we came home on Thursday night."

"So that's why they all went quiet. But Uncle Jeff said no to the pet swap!"

"I know," sighs Frankie, "but secretly he thought it was a good idea and wanted to keep it as another surprise. He just said no to throw Dot off the scent."

"And me!"

"Sorry," sighs Frankie.

Everything starts to make sense now – all the winking and Mum and Dad knowing I was sleeping at Dot's and… "So it was planned! Uncle Jeff did trick me!"

"What's that?" asks Fabio, peeping his head around Frankie's door.

"Nothing," I giggle.

"Fantastico," says Fabio, "because it's time for lunch."

☆   ☆   ☆

Fabio serves up a yummy feast, followed by an extra large slice of died-and-gone-to-heaven chocolate cake!

"He's a good cook," laughs Frankie, as we go back to her room, "but he's absolutely useless at keeping secrets. He was warned not to tell me about Dot's bedroom, but he's SO hopeless he told me everything before we got home! Mum said if I told you, and you told Dot, then the hamsters were mine for ever and ever. And I SO WANTED TO SWAP THEM FOR RABBITS! They fidget all night and … and I know you don't like their scaly feet and they make you nervous when you're in my room… And I thought that if Dot had the hamsters then maybe you'd be nervous in HER ROOM and then you'd want to spend more time in mine."

153

I am totally shocked. "Y-y-you did that for me?"

"Of course," grins Frankie. "You're my best-ever friend. My ÷BEST÷ and ONLY best-ever friend!"

"Your best and only? But you've got a new friend. And don't say you haven't because I've got watertight proof."

"What watertight proof?"

"Nero Minelli."

"Nerd?!" squeals Frankie. "When were you ever talking to him?"

"Last night, when I phoned YOU, only you were too busy with your new best friend to remember you were going to phone ME!"

"*Bird-brain!*" cries Frankie. "I was on my way to Dot's! Your cling-on cousin is my new friend. Well not really. I had to PRETEND because I was so desperate to get rid of my hamsters!"

"Dot's your new friend? Not Brainiac Jenny?"

"Jenny?" laughs Frankie. "You must be joking! And it was SO boring being friends with a cling-on!"

For the rest of the afternoon we play

Twister and gyrate on a dance mat and Frankie says I can stay the night, to make up for her not telling me things.

I'm so tired, what with the dancing and two late nights, and I really wanted to crack the code BUT I'm so happy that she's still my friend, and I'm her only best-ever friend … that I know I have to stay.

Fabio treats us to a spaceship-sized pizza with extra large everything you can ever imagine.

And after four dollops of strawberry ice cream, drizzled with cream and chocolate sauce, we finally settle ourselves in bed (which is a giant bouncy inflatable mattress with two spotty quilts).

"I know," giggles Frankie. "We could get undercover and solve the code. I know how much you want to beat Jenny."

"Thanks," I tell her, "but I'm so tired, I couldn't even add up two and two. But I was just wondering ... how long have you known about my secret? About me not liking scaly things."

"Oh, that," giggles Frankie. "From our first day at school when Trevor chased you with a big fat worm. Plus you'll never go in the pet shed, yet you like rabbits and dogs and cats, and the only difference between them and hamsters is their furry, not scaly feet."

"Oh," I whisper. "I never even knew that you knew. Is that why you slept in front of the hamsters last night?"

"Thought you wouldn't sleep a wink if I didn't..."

"Thanks," I sigh. "And guess what? ...WE'VE BEEN SAVED BY A CLING-ON!"

And we both laugh as we think of Dot all tucked up in her new fairy bedroom with her scaly-footed friends.

"She's not so bad really," sighs Frankie.

"Mmmmm," I yawn. "Not as bad as garlic snails

... but not as good as sleeping! Night-night, Frankie. Friends forever?"

"Of course!" giggles Frankie. "For ever and ever!"

SUNDAY

Watercress soup & my genius dad!

"Well?" says Mum, when I get back home.

"Well what?" I ask. (I know exactly, precisely just what she means, but two can play at keeping secrets.)

"Did Dotty like her little surprise?"

"LITTLE!" I squeal. "It was the BIGGEST surprise in the whole of the universe."

"I know," laughs Mum. And she winks at Dad, who is sat on the floor with Spike in his arms, and Dad giggles and winks back.

"OK, you can stop that now," I tell them. "The surprises are over. And you should have told me. I'm good at secrets."

"Sorry," says Mum, "but we had to have someone to distract Dot ... and everyone agreed that you'd be perfect. We didn't tell you because we needed you to act normally so that Dotty wouldn't suspect a thing. It was hard enough to manage as it was, but you're such a brilliant undercover puzzler, Minnie, that we thought we'd use you as a kind of suspicious measuring device."

"A suspiciousometer," giggles Dad, "and we knew that if YOU weren't suspicious then we were safe with Dot."

"A suspiciousometer! But I WAS SUSPICIOUS! I was totally suspicious!"

"Oh," sighs Dad. "Gran thought you might be. And talking of Gran, she came round earlier with a book you might like. I've put it on your bed."

"Bed!" glugs Spike, as I give him a cuddle.

"Someone wants their lunch," chuckles Dad.

"Not me," I tell him. "I've eaten so much at Frankie's house I feel like I might burst!"

"Lucky thing," whispers Dad, as Mum heads for the kitchen. "Me and Spike are stuck with watercress soup. And it looks like something from a witch's cauldron!"

"I heard that!" shouts Mum.

"Must be those witch's ears," laughs Dad. "If I was you I'd escape now, Minnie Minx!"

☆   ⭐   ☆

On my bed is the book from Gran and a tiny present, and a note saying, "Present from Aunty Valerie, codebook from me. Read page ten very carefully."

I sit on the floor and unwrap the present and there inside, is a slide for my hair and it has three purple hearts all in a row. Frankie will be jealous, but I might let her borrow it and I pin it in my hair and climb into bed and go undercover to read Gran's book. It is all about punctuation in all the wrong places, which is just like Mr Impey's message, and it gives an example and tells you to try an example yourself.

I study what to do and make up a message to send to Frankie, and then I follow the rules and, after some particularly tricky thinking, I write...

FAKE IEYUOTIIE LIGA!R NI, BT O7P
RXBL ASRN

And there is punctuation in all the wrong places! So far, so good, and what you must do next is count the letters and punctuation marks, and put the first half on a top line and the second half on a bottom line and then it will look like this...

F A K E I E Y U O T I I E L I G A !
R N I , B T O 1 p R X B L A S R N

And if you join the letters diagonally up and down like this…

…it says…

F RANKIE, I BET YoU 10p TRIXIBELLA
IS GRAN !

And now the weird punctuation makes perfect sense!

I try it on Mr Impey's message, but after pickling my brain for nearly an hour all it annoyingly says is…

vppLmphitmsFyvip;osmypompympdLepjg
pyrjbrrvt;uppvilsntury/jgrpntpnsrtofm/h
hdppssvm;frhbrrytosym/fovytosdvulpoimt
hDyRjVrTvRpYfSrHyRjMrYt[rtoodxsry/e

So I take a break and come out of my room, and there is Spike, caterpillar green from top to toe in Mum's disgusting watercress soup.

"Better out than in," giggles Dad. "I wish I could have tipped mine on my head!"

I look for Mum, but she's out shopping, so I sit in front of a blank TV and Dad joins me and says, "Penny for them, Minnie Minx. 1p if you tell me what you're thinking."

"10p and it's a deal."

"20p, but you have to dress Spike, and that includes putting his nappy on!"

"No way!"

And Dad gives up and goes to change Spike, and I'm still dreaming in front of the TV when he comes back and sits at his desk with Spike bouncing between his knees. Then he turns on the computer to write a letter, which is not a good idea as Dad has fingers that can't type and Mum usually does it for him, so I take my chances and offer, "I'll type it for 50p."

"You're on," nods Dad, as he hands me a handwritten letter to copy. "Thanks, Minnie. I hate typing. I just keep hitting the wrong buttons. And now I know why they call it a keyboard. It's because it's go-to-sleep-mind-dimmingly boring to type on! I'm going to call it a..." And I'm just waiting for one of his jokes when I watch him tap out...

And as the letters appear on the screen, my mind starts to swirl with secret-code thoughts. And suddenly...

KEY... BORED!

"Dad!" I shriek. "I think you've cracked it! You've found the answer to cracking the code!"

"I have?" laughs Dad. "I didn't feel a thing!"

And for once I laugh at his terrible joke and giggle, "Dad, I think you're a genius! A code-cracking genius! Mum was right ... I should never underestimate you. You really are mastermind clever!"

"Minnie Piper, did I just hear you say Dad is clever?" grins Mum, as she staggers in with the shopping.

"Totally," I squeal. "It's his speciality.

HE'S ONLY CRACKED THE SECRET CODE!"

"He has?" laughs Mum. "What does it say?"

"I'm just about to find that out. But first I need to type Dad's letter."

"Don't worry!" says Dad. "Mum's back now. And I'll still give you 50p if you crack the code."

"Thanks, Dad! I'm so excited I'd probably type it wrong anyway. My hands won't stop shaking!" And I can't wait to get started and I stare at the keyboard and copy down its letters in my dolphin notebook, just as they appear, in three long rows...

```
QWERTYUIOP []
ASDFGHJKL;'#
ZXCVBNM,./
```

And I go to my room and climb under my duvet and open my dolphin notebook and like an undercover puzzler I begin to jot.

And it takes me for ever but this time I know that I am totally, definitely, 100% RIGHT!

And not only can I read the secret message, but I've super-sleuthingly WON £2.00!

I telephone Gran, because I'm absolutely bursting to tell her, and Gran says, "Well done, dear, I always knew you were a puzzling bee. You'd better tell me all about it."

BUzzzzz
Buzz

And I explain about the computer keyboard, and instead of being surprised, and not understanding (because Gran is not computer savvy) she says, "Ah yes, I should have known. They had something like that in the war, dear. Enigma it was called, and that had a keyboard…"

"…And when you tapped in one letter a different letter secretly lit up! Gran, you're so clever! Mr Impey taught us all about it. I was going to tell you and then I forgot." Gran laughs and says she'll bake me a chocolate cake for a code-cracking celebration tea.

And then I phone Frankie and she whoops really loudly and says, "I knew you were cleverer than Brainiac Jenny!"

☆   ☆   ☆

I go to Gran's for tea and her chocolate cake is almost as lip-smacking as Fabio Minelli's. And when it's time to go home, I go to bed and tap on my wall for Wanda Wellingtons, and like a secret agent she peeps her head around my door and I tap my duvet three times and she jumps up and licks my face before curling up at the bottom of my quilt. And, as soon as I've uttered, "I've done it, Wanda. I've cracked the code," we both fall fast asleep.

And tonight I dream…

…Mr Impey is bouncing up and down like a trampoliner saying, "Minnie Piper, you are spookily brilliant at cracking the code and have won the puzzler's undercover prize!"

MONDAY

Hands up!

I wake up to Dad warning me that my Rice Krispies are turning to frogspawn and I begin to panic that it's all been a dream, and I've not truthfully solved the code. But just in case, I cross my fingers and look under my mattress, and there it is … my prize-winning evidence, all written down in my notebook!

I have never been so excited to go to school and I feel so dizzy that I put my sweatshirt on inside out and I don't even notice that my socks don't match, or that I'm eating Dad's cornflakes and not my Rice Krispies. In fact I'm so happy that I don't even care about my poodle hair and, instead of tying it as tight as I can, I leave it loose, except for Aunty Valerie's purple slide.

But all the dizziness makes me late because I forget my lunch and I have to turn back, just on the day that I need to be early.

"Good afternoon, Minnie," teases Mr Impey, as I finally make it into class. I am desperate to tell him I've cracked the code, but there's no time as assembly is starting and the rest of the class are all in the hall. I have to sneak in with Mr Impey and together we stand right at the back and Grumpy is droning on about looking smart … and looking right at me!

"He was looking at me," I whisper to Mr Impey, when assembly is over and we file out.

"No he wasn't," chuckles Mr Impey. "He was looking at me!"

And I look at him in his emerald-green tracksuit, a little bit like a giant grasshopper and say, "But I can't imagine you in smart clothes."

"Thanks, Minnie," he smiles. "I'll take that as a compliment."

"But Mr Impey," says Tiffany, "Minnie's got her jumper on inside out!"

And everyone laughs, apart from Frankie, who is busy mouthing, "WHERE HAVE YOU BEEN?"

"I forgot my lunch." And we turn into class and go to our seats and Mr Impey says, "Right then, Chickenpoxers, who's going to tell me about their weekend?"

Jenny and I shoot up our hands, and I twitch and panic and my confidence drains, as suddenly I realize that I'm not the only one who has cracked the code. Brainiac Jenny has done it as well! And horror of horrors, Mr Impey is picking her first! I look at Frankie, and Frankie immediately waves her hand and shouts, "Minnie has fabaroony news, Mr Impey!"

"That's nice," smiles Mr Impey. "She can tell us all in just a jiffy. Now Jenny, what have you got to share with the class?"

"But Mr Impey!"

"You're next, Frankie."

And that's it, despite Frankie's efforts, my moment of glory (that I've been practising since Sunday teatime) is lost to Brainiac Jenny. And I shouldn't be jealous because she doesn't have a best-ever friend like me who will wave their hand in the air to save her, BUT I AM JEALOUS. I'M TOTALLY JEALOUS and I stuff my fingers into my ears so I don't have to hear a word she says. But it doesn't work, and whilst Frankie is crossing her fingers for luck (plus her arms and knees and eyes), I hear every single spooky word...

"My mum's having another baby!"

And that's it! No code! No nothing! WHAT KIND OF NEWS IS THAT?

And Mr Impey says, "That's lovely, Jenny."

And Tiffany says, "That means Jenny will have six brothers and sisters!"

And I try to imagine having six Spikes, all dribbling and wriggling like tadpoles when, "Well go on, *Bird-brain!*" whispers Frankie. "It's finally your big moment!"

And everyone watches as I take my chair and put it by the clock, by the side of the board, and, as Trevor heckles, "Blinkin' bonkers Minnie Piper!" I proudly retrieve a £2.00 coin that is so shiny it could have been polished by Arthurs Way fairies!

Frankie is cheering, "Way to go, *Poodle Noodle!*"

And Mr Impey is clapping and saying, "Well done, Minnie! You've cracked the code! I was beginning to think that no one would do it. Perhaps you can tell us all how you did it."

"OK," I grin, sticking my £2.00 coin on my desk.

And I open my notebook and copy the code on to the board.

vpmhtsyi: sy opmd ejprbrt
upi str/ gpt nromh dp
v;rbrt smf vtsvlomh yjr
ypfr yjrtr od s yep [pimf vpom
pm yp[pg yjr v;pvl nu
yjr npstf/hp smf hry oy/
oy od upit DRVTRY SHRMY [toxr/

And beneath the code I copy out the letters from a computer keyboard.

QWERTYUIOP [ ]
ASDFG HJKL;'#
ZXCVBNM,./

I look at Frankie, who is looking at me, and grinning like a cat from ear to ear, and say, "The first clue was 'the key to the code is being bored', and this was Mr Impey's secret way of saying that we would find the answer on a KEYBOARD." And I very neatly write:

KEY BORED !

Trevor groans and I can see Jenny looking slightly gutted and Tiffany Me-Me says, "But that's not fair because my brothers are always on our computer at home and they never let me use it!"

"That isn't fair," agrees Mr Impey, "but we do have computers in school, Tiffany." And Tiffany sulks and chews her nails.

And I keep on explaining, even though I am totally shaking. "And the second clue was learning about Enigma. That was about making codes with a keyboard too, and hitting one letter and getting another."

"Well done, Minnie," grins Mr Impey. "So what do we do when we have our keyboard?"

"Easy!" I beam. "Follow your third clue, which was to think backwards! A simple way to crack a code is to work back one letter in the alphabet so that all the C's in the message are really B's and all the B's are really A's. But for this secret message we work back one letter on the keyboard!"

"Fabiozo!" cheers Frankie.

"Excellent!" cries Mr Impey. And he hops up and down like the giant green grasshopper he appears to be and cries, "Ten more marbles for the Chickenpox marble pot! Now, before secret-agent Minnie tells us all the answer, why don't you try and work it out for yourselves… Well go on then, what are you waiting for?"

Ten minutes later...

"Minnie," whispers Frankie. "Swap you some died-and-gone-to-heaven chocolate cake for the answer!"

"Plus a slice of pizza?" I bargain back.

"OK." And, spy-in-a-raincoat-and-dark-glasses secretly, she gives me a wink and a nod of the head.

And, fingers crossed, like an undercover-puzzler I slip her my notebook...

"Thanks," laughs Frankie. "Best friends forever!"

"For ever and ever," I giggle back.

Congratulations
whoever you are.
For being so clever
and cracking the code
there is a two pound
coin on top of the
clock by the board.

Go and get it.
☆ It is your ☆
SECRET AGENT prize.

DEI · GRATIA · REGINA
ELIZABETH · II · F · D